Too Scared to Sleep

ANDREW DUPLESSIE

CLARION BOOKS
An Imprint of HarperCollins *Publishers*

Clarion Books is an imprint of HarperCollins Publishers.

Too Scared to Sleep
Text copyright © 2023 by Alloy Entertainment LLC

Produced by Alloy Entertainment
30 Hudson Yards, 22nd Floor, New York, New York 10001

www.epicreads.com

Library of Congress Cataloging-in-Publication Data
Names: Duplessie, Andrew, author.
Title: Too scared to sleep / Andrew Duplessie.
Description: First edition. | New York : Clarion Books, an imprint of HarperCollins
    Publishers, [2023] | Audience: Ages 13 up. | Audience: Grades 10-12. |
    Summary: A collection of spooky short stories.
Identifiers: LCCN 2022052146 | ISBN 9780063266483 (hardcover)
Subjects: CYAC: Horror stories. | Short stories. | LCGFT: Horror fiction. | Short
    stories.
Classification: LCC PZ7.1.D8685 To 2023 | DDC [Fic]—dc23
LC record available at https://lccn.loc.gov/2022052146

Typography by Alice Wang
23 24 25 26 27 LBC 5 4 3 2 1

First Edition

CONTENTS

IF YOU ARE READING THIS BOOK,
MAKE SURE YOU ARE NOT NEAR
ANY ELECTRICAL DEVICES.

THEY ARE WATCHING.

AND LISTENING.

Inside your bedroom is good. Under your covers is even better.

Have you ever heard the saying "Truth is stranger than fiction"? Well, the best stories contain truth. Truth is why I write this book. Every story that follows is true. Mostly terrifying, often shocking, always truthful. The only details I've changed are names and locations, to protect those who told me their stories—the ones still alive, that is. This book is a warning, a glimpse into our dark future.

Over the last few months, I've received a lot of advice suggesting that I don't share these stories with you. That's why we're going old-school, analog, cover to cover. A book is the only place that's safe.

Read this book and pass it around to your friends, so they can be warned too.

You never know when the darkness is coming for you.

SHORT FRIGHTS FOR DARK NIGHTS

....

I know you don't want to hear it, but ghosts are real.
That shadow in the corner of your eye? It moved. And
your favorite teddy bear? Well, sometimes it's watching.

WASTE MANAGEMENT

"Dad!" Casey yelled. "The stupid disposal is jammed again."

She leaned forward and scowled down the drain. It was burbling something brownish, chunky. She wrinkled her nose. It had been coughing up the same nasty gunk for days. Whatever it was, it was all over the edges of the sink and counter, like dried-on pizza sauce.

No matter how much she yelled up the stairs, her father never came down to deal with it.

"It's super gross," she added, still hollering. "Smells like old hot dogs."

Casey's phone buzzed on the kitchen counter beside her. She snatched it up and grinned at her best friend's name flashing across the notifications. Her mind emptied instantly, like an upturned drawer.

She didn't notice the disposal still churning and sputtering. If her father had bothered to walk downstairs, he would've started lecturing her about breaking the motor.

It's an old house, he always said. *An old system. You gotta take care of it, or it'll come back to bite 'cha.*

Laina: Basketball team capt at westlake is throwing this huge party tonight

The disposal glugged and growled. It vomited up a chip of something whitish, like a bit of chicken bone.

Casey's eyes glowed with delight, but they stayed locked on her screen.

Casey: Serious?
Laina: And someone's wonderful smart best friend got both of us invites
Casey: SERIOUS?

Excitement flared in Casey's belly. No one invited ninth graders to *real* parties.

Laina: ofc im serious 😊 we can come pick u up!
u with ur madre or padre this weekend?

Casey hesitated. She glanced up the stairs. Her father was probably up there working on some five-million-piece puzzle or carving another crappy wooden duck. If she went up there and asked, he would start lecturing her about chores and boys and her turn to make dinner.

As if reading her mind, he groaned down the stairs, "Feed me, Casey. I'm so hungry."

Reason number 52,000 it was better at her mom's house, where they had the unspoken agreement to sit on their phones and totally ignore each other. Where, when Casey went out, her mom only ever said, "Have fun!"

Casey's mind spun with an idea: She could make up a big project for her history class and tell her dad she was going to the library or something stupid like that. Something her dad would approve of.

The garbage disposal growled, guttural, hungry.

Her father's voice echoed through the house. "Feed me."

Casey: I'm at the dictator's house and i have to pay him respects in the form of dinner before he kills my dreams

Laina shot back a GIF of a woman covering her mouth, trying not to laugh.

The disposal glug-glugged more. She rolled her eyes and left it on. At least if it was a hundred percent broken, her dad would actually fix it—and maybe clean up his mess while he was at it.

"Hey, Dad, I'm going to the library with Laina. I'll probably be back late. But I'll put on some, um . . ." Casey opened the fridge door. She scowled until she saw it—a glass jar full of something red. It had the meaty chunks of her dad's usual homemade tomato sauce. "Pasta. I'll put on some pasta. Okay?"

Her father called back, gurgling, "Feeeeed me."

Casey scoffed under her breath, "Rude."

But he just kept going. "Feed me, feeeed me."

Casey leaned against the counter and put in her earbuds to drown out her dad. Soon, Electric Viper's newest album thrummed in her ears. Casey couldn't hear anything as she pulled a pot from the cabinet. She hummed as she popped open her father's spaghetti sauce. Then she froze.

There was a fingernail floating on top.

She glanced back to the thick, red liquid sputtering from the disposal. A pair of yellow eyes stared back at her, rippling under the filthy water.

Casey shrieked and staggered backward.

A pair of rotten arms shot out of the sink. They were slick and mucusy, pocked with old food and rot.

The music was still blaring as those hands dragged her down into the sink. Her cheek slapped against the cold porcelain, her skull like an egg. She heard herself crying, "Dad! Dad, please!"

The voice roared over the music, louder than anything.

"FEED ME!"

When Casey's mother arrived to pick her up the next day, the house was empty. She found Casey's phone on the counter, full of dozens of unread messages, and a pot on the floor.

"Jack?" Casey's mother called. "Casey?"

The garbage disposal was running, puking up something brownish and stinking of rot.

"Jeez, Jack," she said under her breath. "You could keep this place cleaner, you know."

If she had opened the fridge, she would have seen a second jar there, beside the first. It was only half the size. And soon the family would be complete.

Casey's mother reached for the switch on the wall. She was too busy texting her ex-husband to notice the yellow eyes watching her. The ravenous smile made of a dozen people's teeth, wedged in a moldy face.

"I'm hungry," it hissed. "Feed me."

Will you help me?
I'm stuck
You can't?
It's true...
All I really want
Is to be stuck with you

SCAN THE CODE
FOR A SCARE

↓

TOO
SCARED
TO
SLEEP

MR. BUTTERSCOTCH

Sarah hated being grounded more than anything.

She sat in her room, angry and bored, looking for something—anything—to do besides fixate on the crack under her door. It glowed, which meant the kitchen lights were on. Her parents were still up, so she was still banished to her room.

Sarah paused, considering her options. Her parents would certainly be angry if she left her room now. They had already grounded her for texting at the dinner table and had taken her phone. She didn't dare risk making it worse. Never mind that she was fourteen and being sent to her room was totally humiliating. Having a phone was her social lifeline. She could practically feel the dozens of unanswered messages calling to her from the other room.

The minutes ticked by, and her anger turned to boredom. What was she supposed to even *do*?

She hadn't opened her toy crate since she was a young girl, but tonight was not the night to be mature. She was phoneless, lonely, and bored. She lifted the latch up on the mangled old box and dug through the piles of stuffed animals. Their plastic eyes winked at her in the low light. Many of them were more disfigured than she remembered, but the one she was looking for—her stuffed rabbit, Mr. Butterscotch—was sitting right on top with a big smile stitched onto his face. The same smile that had always cheered her up whenever she was down. His fur was worn, revealing the spots where he had served as a tissue for her tears.

He'd been a gift on her second birthday, and after that they were inseparable—he was her favorite toy and her closest friend. Sarah brought Mr. Butterscotch with her everywhere: to the doctor, the store, sometimes even to movies. As long as Mr. Butterscotch was with her, she felt safe and happy.

But Sarah grew up. She made friends at school. She got a phone. Nowadays, she spent her evenings hanging out with her friends online or texting. Sarah didn't need him anymore. She'd put him in her toy chest and forgotten about him.

But now, grasping him as she always once had, resting her nose on his head in that familiar spot, the fond memories came flooding back. He'd always been the best listener. She sat Mr. Butterscotch on her pillow and let it all tumble out, weeping and telling him how horribly unfair it all was. How she wished she didn't have parents at all. It was nice to vent to *someone*, even if it felt a little childish.

Mr. Butterscotch sat there listening, his beady eyes staring at her and his smile fixed in place. Long after the tears ran dry, Sarah must've dozed off because some time later she jerked awake with a start. In a fog of hunger and confusion, she lifted her head from her pillow. It was three thirty in the morning.

The whole house smelled of freshly roasted meat.

Mr. Butterscotch was nowhere to be seen. Hadn't she left him on her pillow? And why would her parents be cooking at this hour?

Sarah climbed out of bed and pushed open the door. Light spilled in, cutting a yellow crease across her bedroom floor. Her stuffed animals seemed to raise their fleecy paws in good luck or goodbye. She blinked hard and squinted into the darkness, and they were immobile statues once more. Her mind must've been playing tricks on her.

She crept down the hall. The honey-sweet scent of fat cooking grew stronger as she tiptoed into the empty kitchen. She turned her head this way and that, looking for shapes in the gloom. Signs of her parents.

All the lights in the house were dead except for the kitchen. Even the dining room adjacent to the kitchen was dark, except for a tidy row of candles set up among a feast of covered silver trays. Her mother's finest dishware. Sarah hadn't seen it used since her grandmother died.

But there it was, laid out in the middle of the night, like a feast for ghosts.

Sarah hugged her arms over her chest. She peered into the oven. The huge tray her parents always used for Thanksgiving dinner sat in there, covered in a half globe of tinfoil. Hunger tumbled and twisted in her belly.

The oven timer chirped, making Sarah yelp in surprise. She turned, expecting to see her father emerge from the dark to scold her for being out of bed.

But the familiar shape that shuffled closer was too small to be her parents. For a moment, she thought it might be her dog, Daisy, lumbering over to beg for table scraps. But this figure walked upright on two furry back legs, and its tall ears twitched as it hopped along.

"Mr. Butterscotch," Sarah gasped. She almost questioned why he was moving on his own, but she stifled that impulse. Obviously, this was just a dream. "What are you doing out of bed?" she asked instead.

"You missed out on dinner." Her stuffed animal flopped up

to her with ragdoll looseness. He looked sweet and silly, his little stitched mouth smiling up at her. "So I made you one."

"Oh, you kind old rabbit." She picked him up and cradled him.

Mr. Butterscotch blinked, his eyes flat and unreadable. Something stained the tips of his paws. Perhaps it was sauce from cooking. It reminded her of pennies, but she couldn't quite think of why.

Mr. Butterscotch wriggled out of her arms. He gestured toward the dimly lit dining room table. "Shall we?"

A question lingered in Sarah's gut, poisoning her appetite. She paused. "Where are Mom and Dad?"

The rabbit's stitched lips curled, and for the first time, she saw he had teeth. Little triangles of felt poked out of his smile. "Right here."

Mr. Butterscotch slipped past her and opened the oven door. He pulled out the tray bare-pawed, as if his little furry paws could not feel the blazing heat. He set it on the counter and peeled back the aluminum cover.

Inside, oil sizzled at the bottom of the pan. The scent was unlike anything she had smelled before, rich and sharp in her nose. A shank of meat sat in the tray, steam clouding up off it. A sharp tooth of bone stuck out from the cooked flesh.

The stuffed rabbit gave her another toothy smile. He nodded toward the dining room table.

"Please," he said, "sit down. Our feast is about to begin."

Sarah turned to do as her bunny told her. All of this had the comforting haze of a dream. Surely that's all it was, if her toys were coming to life and speaking to her. That was when a jolt of color caught her eye.

A streak of scarlet smeared the doorframe. It was low, at

eye level, and it, too, smelled like old coins. She leaned to peer down the hall. The door leading to her parents' room hung ajar. The blood smear led past the door, into the darkness beyond.

"Mom?" she whispered. "Dad?"

The room answered with silence. It would be so easy to check to see if they were there. Just nudge the door open, look for the familiar shape of them sleeping in the gloom. But somehow, she knew if she opened the door, there would be no going back.

Sarah dared a glance at Mr. Butterscotch. He was too busy slicing the meat to notice her.

She pinched her own arm hard, willing herself to wake up. But the room around her stayed the same, and the smell of Mr. Butterscotch's feast still dizzied her. It made her woozy. Nauseous.

This was real. The blood on her parents' door was real.

Her stuffed rabbit puttered around the kitchen, whistling happily. "Should I put some juice on the table?"

Sarah's pulse quickened as she gingerly pulled open a utensil drawer and reached in to grab the sharpest knife she could find. A dull steak knife. Not much, but it would have to do. She held it behind her back.

"I don't think my mom and dad would like that. They said I shouldn't have sugar late at night."

"We don't have to worry about what they think. Not tonight. This is our feast."

Mr. Butterscotch skipped past her to put the tray of meat on the table. "Shall we eat? You must be hungry."

Indignation tightened Sarah's throat. She gripped the knife tighter, only her hand was slippery from sweat. "Not yet."

Her stuffed animal hopped to the table, his ears bobbing

with a looseness she used to find endearing. But now there was a menace to it. What was that phrase her mother told her? A wolf in sheep's clothing.

Mr. Butterscotch didn't seem to notice her pause. He set the last serving tray on the table. "Come along, Sarah," he chided. "Your dinner is going to get cold." He impaled a sliver of meat on a fork and slapped it onto the closest plate.

Sarah couldn't bring herself to move. "Not until my mom and dad are here."

Now the toy rabbit started giggling to himself. In a warped and delighted voice, he said, "Silly girl, they're already here!"

He leaned over to the center serving tray, her mother's finest silver. He wrapped a bloody paw around it and lifted the lid.

Her mother's head stared back at her, mirroring Sarah's shock in her lifeless eyes. Steam rose from the wrinkled, cooked skin overlying those once-familiar features.

Sarah held the knife even tighter. She swallowed the urge to vomit.

Mr. Butterscotch watched her hungrily. "Now, sit down," he said in a wheezing, singsong voice. "Or join your parents there."

Sarah shuffled closer. She sat down slowly.

"Go on. Give your mother a taste." The rabbit leaned in, its button eyes glowing with unholy delight in the light of the chandelier. "After all, you said you wished you didn't have parents."

Bile rose in Sarah's mouth. She swung out with the knife. The dull blade caught and tore the fabric flesh of the rabbit's belly. Cotton spilled out of the open wound.

The bunny looked between her and the knife in mild surprise.

"Oh dear," Mr. Butterscotch said. "It seems you've chosen to join the feast, but not in the way I had hoped. Then again, you've always been selfish, Sarah. Casting others aside when you're finished with them. After everything we've been through, and for what? To be replaced by a screen? I'd hoped we could start again, but now it's time for you to get a taste of your own medicine."

"Wait—" Sarah tried.

But the rabbit lunged, arcing a fork toward her throat, silencing her forever.

The house smelled of meat long into the morning.

Is there a better disguise
Than your bunny
With the cute button eyes
What if that bunny has fears
About how you've changed
Through the years
And no longer listens to your cries
And no longer cares about your tears

SCAN THE CODE
FOR A SCARE

THE SECRET SISTER

There was a girl living in Emma's bedroom wall.

Emma had heard her the first night they moved in. It started as a faint tapping against the interior of the brick wall beside her bed. She pressed her ear to it and listened long into the night.

Emma had been only nine then, and her imagination was alive with ghost stories. After all, the house was an old Victorian that hunched over like an elderly woman.

It was exactly the kind of place a ghost would live. Surely it was haunted.

When Emma told her parents that morning over breakfast, her father said, "Probably just the pipes."

"Or rats," Emma's mother added. She didn't even glance up from her phone, on which she always read the morning news. Murder and war, there at the breakfast table. "The old lady who owned this place last didn't take the best care of it."

Emma's father grinned and gestured at the peeling, mold-blackened wallpaper with his toast. "Case in point."

But it wasn't rats, and it wasn't pipes. Because over the next few years, Emma woke up almost every night to the sound of a little girl singing.

And then one night, when Emma had just turned fourteen, she started to talk. It was the faintest whisper, but unmistakable. "Please," she whispered. "Please talk to me."

Emma rolled over. Her heart thrummed against her ribs as she said, "Is someone there?"

"Yes," came the answer, quiet and full of despair. "I've always been here."

"Who are you? How did you get in there?"

"I'm Nancy. I don't remember how I got here. It's been so long. I just—I want a friend."

Emma gulped and got out of bed. She walked to the spot on the wall where she'd heard a scratching sound—*scritch, scritch*—and the brick came loose.

Two green eyes stared back at her.

"We could be friends," Emma told her with a smile. "I'm Emma."

The two girls stayed up talking all that night and the next and the next, until they finally fell asleep from exhaustion. It was like having a secret sister. They made up little games, trying to guess where one would tap next on the brick. Emma told her about what it was like being a girl who went to school, played volleyball, and had friends and crushes. And Nancy drank it all in: the friend drama, the intrigue, even play-by-plays of Emma's recent games. You see, Nancy couldn't leave her room. It was a lonely existence, even for a ghost.

One night, Emma asked her a burning question, the same one she had asked that first night. "How did you get stuck in there?"

"Well," Nancy said, carefully. "The last thing I remember is playing hide-and-seek with my sister. There was once a door on this wall. I opened it up and climbed inside. But then the door disappeared. Like the house . . . ate it. And I've been trapped here ever since. I didn't die, at least I don't think so. I'm just . . . stuck."

Questions spiraled around Emma's mind. She wondered how a house could eat a girl, trapping her there forever. She also wondered how long she had been in there. Why had she stopped aging? And why didn't she know anything about the outside world? She'd never even heard of cell phones or the internet or the surround-sound speakers Emma's parents were installing in the living room.

The next morning, on the drive to school, Emma asked her father, "What was the name of the old woman who used to live here?"

Her father's eyes remained trained on the road. "Something Langley, I think. Why, sweetheart?"

"Just curious," Emma said, staring straight ahead.

She knew better than to mention the girl in the wall. Her parents thought she was too old to believe in ghosts.

But when Emma searched on the school computers, she found a newspaper archive from a hundred years ago. And sure enough, there was an article from the local newspaper about a girl named Nancy Langley, who disappeared one day, never to be seen again.

"Emma," Nancy whispered. "Can I ask you something?"

It was the night before Emma's fifteenth birthday.

"Okay, but I'm really tired. I have to go to sleep soon."

"I know. I know tomorrow is a big night. It's just—"

Emma sat up and forced a smile. Tomorrow all her friends were coming over for a party and spending the night. She'd have to put the brick back in the wall to hide Nancy. She'd have to hide her teddy bear, Fuffy, too. She didn't want anyone to make fun of her.

But for tonight, Emma held her teddy close and pressed her ear to the wall to hear her secret sister.

Nancy's voice was a whisper: "Do you think I could come to your party?"

Emma paused and frowned. "But how? Everyone will think I'm a weirdo if I start talking to a wall. No offense."

"I have a theory. I think—" Her voice thickened, and she swallowed hard. "If you touch me . . . maybe I can become real again."

Emma stared at Nancy's pale hand emerging from the hole in the wall. Her fingers looked swollen and old. Like Emma's grandmother's at her funeral.

"How long have your hands been that way?" Emma asked, trying to hide her grimace. She gulped. She'd never touched a ghost before, and the idea made her queasy. But then Emma reminded herself: *She's not just a ghost. She's my friend. She's like a sister. If there's a way I can help her, I have to try.*

Nancy voice was even smaller now. "I'm sorry. I shouldn't have asked."

"No, it's okay." Emma slowly reached toward her swollen, dead-looking hand. "You know I'd do anything to help you."

Emma closed her eyes and wrapped her hand around the cold fingers. Ice shot up her arm. She felt like she'd turned to stone.

Suddenly she was surrounded by darkness. The room felt stuffy and the air heavy, hot. Emma reached for the light switch but found nothing but wall. Her hands inched along the coarse brick looking for anything. Then she spun around, ready to scream.

Light filtered in through a hole in the brick wall.

Light coming from Emma's own bedroom.

Nancy's eyes appeared at the hole in the wall, dark green and full of apologies.

"Nancy," Emma gasped. "What did you do?"

"You have to understand," Nancy said. "I was in there for a

hundred years. I couldn't take it anymore."

Emma fell back against the brick wall and pushed and pushed, but it wouldn't give. And then she pictured it: Nancy reaching for some other kid's hand. Trying to help them. Finding herself here, on the wrong side of the wall.

"You knew," Emma spat out. "You knew."

Emma shoved her fingers back through the wall, but Nancy had already moved away. Emma stared through the gap: Nancy's clothes were filthy gray, covered in cobwebs. She was at Emma's desk now, squeezing craft glue over the brick chunk, frowning.

"You'll understand, Emma. In time. The adults can't hear us because they don't believe. But when some other kid comes along, whenever they do, however long you've been in there, you'll know I had no other choice."

Emma kicked at the wall and screamed for her parents. Tears streaked down her cheeks.

"I'm sorry," Nancy said.

And then she pressed the brick back into place, leaving Emma in darkness.

SCAN THE CODE
FOR A SCARE

⬇

A Riddle

I cannot be heard, cannot be seen
I'm in the stars and everywhere between
Before you wake up and after you lay
You can never dream me away.
What am I?

BEAR TRAP

Heather was nearly two days' deep into the forest when the bear trap got her.

When she felt the give underfoot, she staggered and threw her weight back, but not fast enough. It caught her just above the top of her hiking boot. A mouthful of cruel rusty teeth gouged into her leg. The metal hit her bone so hard, it seemed to rattle her whole body.

Heather fell silent, inhaling her scream. The pain was beyond screaming, beyond feeling itself. She knew it was there, but her mind wouldn't let her get a good grip on it. Maybe that kind of pain would make someone insane. Or maybe it was just the bow-hunter instincts her dad had taught her: Stay quiet. Don't scare off the deer.

So she seethed against her fist and made inventory. Heat lapped up her leg, cresting like a wave.

What did she have? A decent Leatherman multi-tool, her hunting knife, her compound bow, a quiver of arrows, a gallon of water, some jerky, and a satellite phone. Each item had such a different weight four days ago when Heather was packing her bag.

Her friend Claire had looked at her uncertainly. "Are you sure you should go by yourself?"

"Claire," she'd said, insulted. "Don't you think I know what I'm doing?"

Truthfully, there was little Claire might've said that would've stopped her. Both her parents were gone for a week on a second honeymoon to Argentina. She was supposed to stay at Claire's house, but Heather had a different idea. She planned to camp out in the woods behind her house for a full week, which extended back for miles, totally alone like they do on the survivor shows. She was tired of being too young, too small, too weak, too ugly to do or be anyone cool. She wanted to prove to everyone—and herself—that she could do something totally on her own. Something most people couldn't do.

"I don't know . . ." Claire said, uneasy.

"Claire, relax. I know those woods inside and out. I'm not going to die." Heather had said it almost sarcastically.

Now the irony wasn't lost on her.

Heather pawed through her bag until she found her phone, safe in its waterproof case. Furious tears stung at her eyes. She'd planned for everything. She knew what she was doing. She practically grew up in these mountains, hunting every fall with her dad. Something like this couldn't happen to her.

She flicked on the phone. NO SIGNAL.

Blood oozed down the bear trap's terrible jagged teeth. It looked eerily purple in the thick shade of the pines. There was a steel cable slip-knotted around the trap's edge. The wire had been pressed into the dirt and fastened to the exposed root of a nearby tree. Some hunter must have set this decades ago and forgot. She cursed under her breath.

Heather grimaced down at the trap. The tiniest movement made fresh pain bolt up her leg. She pried at the trap, but she could only wedge it open a millimeter or two before her strength failed. That pain did make her scream, and for a while she let herself lay among the dead pine needles and sob.

Sweat dripped over her nose—the kind of sweat that came from pain, not heat. The evening air had already turned chilly, and the beads of sweat soon felt like ice. Shivers sailed down her spine, sending goose bumps in their wake.

She should have stopped and made camp half an hour earlier when she saw the light fading, but she wanted to make it a full three miles before nightfall.

Because she could do it herself. She could do anything.

Heather laughed, because if she didn't laugh she would cry.

For a few hours, she worked at the cable with her Leatherman, but she only managed to dent her pliers. It was cold, but she couldn't feel it. Her whole body was hot and pulsing, damp with sweat.

Heather chewed numbly at beef jerky and sipped water. She rested without sleeping. She heard a mountain lion scream somewhere in the night. That kept her up a long while, wondering if she would rather die in slow delirium or fast panic. Wondering if she'd have the choice.

The second day, she didn't let herself worry. She had water still. She had food. She could dig holes in the clay with her fingers when she needed the bathroom, then bury it again. It wasn't cute, but it worked.

Her foot was so swollen, it pressed against the sides of her boot. Her flesh puffed out over the teeth, like an embedded dog collar.

Claire would notice her absence by now. Two days in a row without an "I'm still alive" call from her phone. She would call her parents, search and rescue. They were probably already out looking for her right now.

On the third day, she told herself she still believed it. But she ate slower, nibbling. She took water in sips. She murmured into the phone like her parents could hear her. "I love you, I'm sorry. I'm sorry."

On the fourth day, she ate and drank nothing. She screamed until her voice broke, and the forest answered her with silence. Flies hummed constantly around her leg, no matter how much she swiped them away. She suddenly understood why cows let them just sit on their eyes.

On the fifth day, Heather woke to a deer snuffling at her backpack. She winced an eye open. The deer's front hoof was beside her head, so close she could reach out and grab it.

"Hey," Heather whispered.

The deer snapped its head toward her and froze like it, too, was surprised she was still alive.

Heather was so delirious with the pain and fever and exhaustion, she was certain the deer could really understand her. That it knew she was dying, and it pitied her.

"You think you could call somebody for me?" she said. And then she started laughing and the deer bolted, crashing through the brush, and was gone.

The world had an uneasy haze to it, like grimy stained glass. Everything was yellow and slanted.

Heather tilted her head and stared at her leg. Here, in the light of a dying world, her leg wasn't her leg. Her body was barely her body. It couldn't feel any worse than this, could it?

Her arm wasn't her arm, so she didn't stop it from reaching into her bag. She didn't stop it from flicking open that hunting knife. Nathan had given it to her for her last birthday. She hadn't even gotten to use it yet.

Heather cut the fabric of her pants away.

Her toes could still wiggle in her hiking boots. Her leg wasn't even that badly broken. If she got to town in time, they could fix it.

No. Not *her* toes. Not *her* leg.

Heather lifted the knife. For hours, she sat there, hunched over. Lifting the knife, lowering the knife. Pressing it against her skin until she drew blood, until the pain was so stinging she stopped and sobbed into her arms.

And on the sixth day, Heather did the only thing she could live with.

She braced the leg that wasn't her leg anymore. She thought of her parents. She thought of twenty stupid yards south, where there was a break in the trees, where she could call for help.

She'd prove to everyone that she could do something they could never do.

Heather lifted the knife.

SCAN THE CODE
FOR A SCARE

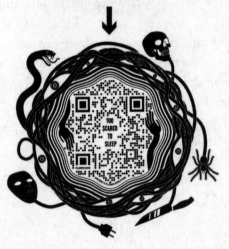

TOO
SCARED
TO
SLEEP

The Bird

There's a bird that only flies east
Driven by the belly of the beast
Through snow, rain, and fire
A growing and growing desire
To hunt, to kill, to feast

THE NIGHTMARE

Elijah woke up earlier than usual. It was still pitch-black outside. The thick darkness syruped his bedroom, except for a strange slit of light that ran from the ceiling to the floor right next to his bed.

It was like a door had been left slightly ajar—but there was no door there. And the light coming through the crack wasn't yellow or white like from a lightbulb. It was crackling ember-red.

Elijah sat up and rubbed his eyes. Then he heard the noise. A ragged breathing type of sound. *Heeeee hoooooo. Heeeeee hoooooo.* As if someone was in his room.

But no one was there.

Elijah swallowed hard and leaned forward as much as he could without falling out of bed. The crack of light still shimmered. And then it changed. For a second—but only a second—he glimpsed another room through the opening.

His heart turned to ice. His body froze.

There was something inside the room beyond.

Eyes.

Someone.

Something.

And it had seen him.

Elijah screamed. He tumbled out of bed, thudding hard onto the carpet.

"Elijah?" came his dad's muffled voice from the hallway.

He'd seen something through the gap. Elijah was certain he had. There had been a red room with a person standing in it peering through the crack. Someone without flesh, with a face that looked sanded off—raw and bloody, without a nose—had been spying on him.

Elijah clawed at the carpet trying to get away. His breath came in ragged pants. Just then, a shadow loomed over him.

Elijah jumped, another scream on the edge of his lips.

"You okay, Eli?"

His dad was by his side now, helping him up.

The slit of light was gone, as if someone had snuffed it out like a candle. Or . . . as if someone had closed the door.

Elijah's father flicked on the bedside lamp. Elijah's room glowed warmly.

He took a few deep breaths as he climbed back into his bed. "There was a doorway. I saw a light through it. And there was . . ."

"It was a dream," said Dad. "Another nightmare. But you're okay. And you need to go back to sleep now because you've got school in the morning."

With the lights on, Elijah could see very clearly that it was just a wall. A plain wall, covered in the jungle-print wallpaper that had been there as long as he could remember.

Just a dream, Elijah thought. Maybe falling out of bed had been the moment he'd really woken up. He'd been having a lot of bad dreams since Mom died.

Elijah frowned. "It just seemed so real."

"Nightmares always seem real, especially in the dark. But no one is there, okay? Now go back to sleep."

"Okay."

"Love you." Dad switched off the light and closed the door.

Elijah leaned back on his pillow and tried to relax.

He'd nearly drifted off again when a thought occurred to him. Why did his dad say no one was there?

He'd only said he'd seen a light.

Elijah switched the lights back on. For some reason, it felt safer that way. For a long while, Elijah watched the door to his bedroom and the spot on his wall where the room beyond had been. Eventually, he slid back down and wrapped his blanket tightly around him.

But Elijah didn't get back to sleep.

And he didn't turn out the lights.

At lunch the next day, Elijah leaned forward over his sandwich and lowered his voice. "I think I'm being watched," he told Ben. They'd been best friends since forever, and Elijah felt like Ben was the only person he could trust with this. "At night. In my room."

"Oh yeah? You got girls peeking through your window, Eli?" Ben raised his brows and smirked.

"No. Not like that. I mean . . . I saw something last night. I don't know what it is, but it's got no skin, like it was all burned off or something."

Ben put down his sandwich and looked sternly at Elijah. "You know you sound crazy, right?"

"I'm not, though. Seriously."

Ben furrowed his brow. "How do you know it wasn't just a nightmare?"

"I was awake, I swear. I heard it." Elijah imitated the sound from last night. *"Heeee hoooooo."*

Ben laughed. "I'll sleep over tonight. You can introduce me to the boogeyman." Ben wiggled his fingers and said, *"Heeeee hoooooooo,"* in a mocking, over-the-top voice.

Elijah rolled his eyes and tried to hide his embarrassment. Maybe he really was imagining things.

That night, Ben inspected every inch of Elijah's wall.

"See, there's nothing here," said Ben. He let out a long yawn, barely bothering to cover his mouth.

They sat on Elijah's bed, a bag of marshmallows between them. Elijah checked his watch. It was almost one in the morning and, so far, nothing of interest had happened. They'd watched Netflix, played games, talked, and now they were both too tired to do anything other than snack.

"What if . . . What if they know we're still awake?" said Elijah. "What if they don't watch us unless we're sleeping? That's why they're so hard to catch."

Ben yawned again. "So what you're saying is that it's okay for us to go to sleep? You know, to lure them out."

Elijah nodded.

"Cool." Ben struggled into his sleeping bag, smiled, then fell back on the floor with a thud. Seconds later, Elijah could hear the heavy breathing of his sleeping friend.

Elijah lay back on his pillow. He took one last look at the area where the red light had been, then closed his eyes.

But he didn't sleep. He forced himself to stay awake. Maybe Ben didn't believe him, but his idea sounded right. So he faked deep, heavy breathing. If he could make them think he was sleeping, that might be enough.

Minutes passed. Maybe hours. Elijah couldn't tell in his exhausted state. But eventually he heard a sound that sent a shiver down his spine.

Heeee hooooo.

Heeee hooooo.

He opened his eyes just a crack. A red glow bathed the room.

"Ben?" he hissed. "Ben, wake up."

No reply.

Elijah opened his eyes a little more. Ben was gone. Just an empty sleeping bag puddled near Elijah.

But the red light, the crack in reality, was back. Elijah prepared himself to lunge toward it in three, two— "Ahhhh!"

The creak of his bedroom door made him jump.

Dad walked in, face down. Ben trotted in behind Dad. The red light remained.

"He wasn't really asleep," Ben said to Elijah's dad.

"Dad, look, there!" Elijah pointed at the red crack. "Do you see it?"

"Of course I do," said Dad.

But for some reason Dad didn't look surprised. Neither of them did.

"Wait . . . what?" Elijah asked.

Dad sighed and rolled his neck with a crack. "Yes, we both know. And unfortunately for you," he said, "this means the experiment has reached its natural conclusion."

Experiment? Elijah was so confused. What was he talking about?

Dad put a hand to his nose, resting his fingers on it. Then, suddenly, he wrenched his entire nose off his face. The skin tore loudly, like fabric ripping, blood dripping out. Dad—the creature—cocked its head toward Elijah and bared its teeth in a wolfish grin. "That's much better."

Elijah's entire body went numb. His heart started to race. "Dad?"

Elijah tried to stand, to run, but heavy hands pushed him back down onto the bed. He looked up at him, unable to move.

Dad stood there shaking his head. "Stay still, Eli."

Elijah looked desperately to Ben for help. But he didn't look like Ben anymore. He had a skinless face and beady, cruel eyes.

"Now we have an extra set of skin for the next experiment," said Ben.

"Not so fast," Dad said with a chuckle. "We have to peel it off him first."

The creature raised one clawed finger toward Elijah. Elijah screamed uselessly as it grazed his forehead. He could feel it pierce the skin, blood bubble toward the surface.

The last thing Elijah saw was a blinding, shimmering red light.

SCAN THE CODE
FOR A SCARE

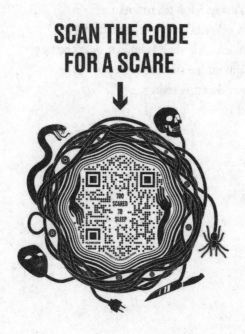

The Monster

If yuo cna rdea thsi then yuo aer not oen of tehm
Thye hvae takne ovre evreythnig
Evreythnig! Nohting si saef!
Thye wtach su
Thye klil su
I cna onyl hlod tehm bakc a ltitle lgoner
Rnu
Rnu away frmo teh mnosetrs
Smoewehre taht teh eivl cnat fnid you
Thye loko lkie rbabits btu aer os muhc wrose
Od nto undreestimtae thme
A nwe dwan is rising.
Rnu!

ANATOMICAL ANOMALIES

....

Bodies are incredible, aren't they? They live, they breathe, they dream . . . they die. In this section you'll find tales about the body that are as scary as they are improbable. Some of them include themes about real-life horrors—like cancer. Proceed with caution.

A Riddle

I am why you cry.
I'm why you scream.
Why you tremble.
Why you beg.
Why you breathe.
And I am your prison.
What am I?

ARE YOU READY?

"Are you ready, Brother?"

Samuel's question sat unanswered as his brother, Lucas, lay beneath a jungle of wires and tubes in a cramped hospital room. His life-support machine beeped steadily, a reminder that he was still alive even if his body refused to show it. The cancer had destroyed him. Samuel knew they didn't have much time left.

"I'm ready," Lucas finally replied. His answer was perfectly clear as it echoed in the halls of Samuel's mind. Being telepathic with his twin seemed like a curse at times, but as Samuel held Lucas's limp hand, communicating with him when no one else could, he knew that their bond was a gift. He treasured it more than anything else.

"Are you scared?" Samuel asked without speaking.

A short pause—then, "A little. But I've been in pain for so long. I can't go on like this anymore. It's time. Tell Mom and Dad how much I love them."

Samuel blinked back tears. "No matter what happens, I'll be here for you. We're a team." Samuel squeezed Lucas's hand and felt a flicker, as though Lucas was trying to squeeze back.

Lucas opened his eyes and gave Samuel a long and weary look. "Do you think it will work? That we'll stay connected once I'm . . . on the other side?" he asked telepathically.

Samuel's jaw tightened. He gave Lucas a short, curt nod. They'd talked about this for months, planned for it. Samuel was certain that nothing could sever their link—not even death.

After all, it had been that way since they were born. Perhaps even before they were born. Why not after?

But Lucas had never been certain. Oftentimes, doubt would creep into Lucas's thoughts like a cancer of its own. Samuel always tried to tune it out. But now, as the familiar doubt sprung up once more in Lucas's mind, it wormed its way into Samuel's mind, too. What if this was the end after all? What if their bond wasn't carried into the afterlife? If there even was an afterlife. The twins would both be alone for the first time in their known existence.

They were about to find out.

Samuel gave Lucas another small reassuring smile, and Lucas's weary, sunken eyes slowly closed. He looked peaceful, and his mind was finally quiet as he flatlined and the alarm sounded, a long beep interrupted only by the soft sniffles of their parents.

Lucas was finally gone.

Samuel turned to his mom and dad, and they folded him into a group hug. "Lucas wanted me to tell you that he loves you both." At this, his mom's sobs became wails. She squeezed Samuel tightly.

His parents knew about their special bond. When they'd been boys, they'd told their secret. At first, their parents didn't believe them, but they'd proven it time and time again. Once, when they were about ten years old, Samuel had been at the grocery store with his mom, and she'd fallen and broken her wrist. Barely a minute later, she'd gotten a phone call from their dad at home. "Lucas says you're hurt." After that, they never questioned it. In fact, it became a special family miracle they'd all vowed to protect.

Now his mother clung to him with desperate eyes. "Is he still there?" she asked. "Is he?"

Samuel didn't dare to test his connection with Lucas for a time. He was afraid of what the answer might be, or that there wouldn't be one at all. But his parents were staring at him through tears, waiting for an answer.

Samuel took a deep breath and worked up the courage. "Brother, can you hear me?"

All he heard was silence.

"Lucas, please—please tell me you're there. I can't lose you."

Still, there was nothing.

"We were supposed to be a team forever. What am I going to do without you?"

Samuel turned to his parents, and his face must have said it all. His mother broke down into a ravaging sob, and his father held her. Samuel went to hold her, too, then—

The pain was blinding. He collapsed to the ground, writhing. He heard himself scream, but it sounded inhumane, like a wild creature. Was that his voice? Was that him? Nothing felt real. He couldn't tell where he was, or even who he was. The only thing he knew for sure was pain.

Eventually, the pain became slightly more familiar, like eyes adjusting to the darkness. He regained feeling in the rest of his body—but his throat didn't hurt. Samuel was able to breathe choppily and even vomited straight onto the floor, but the screaming persisted.

His head felt like it would explode. His eyes seared.

Dad rushed to his side, cupping his face. He was saying something, but Samuel couldn't hear him over the noise. His lips seemed to say, "What's wrong, Samuel?"

It was then that Samuel realized the horrifying truth:

He wasn't the one screaming.

Is that something I smell?
Or could it be the pits of hell
Every day I watch and wait
For what will be my final fate
Ding, ding, ding, the final bell

SCAN THE CODE
FOR A SCARE

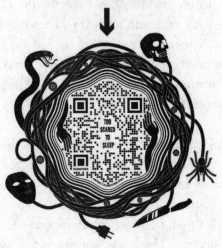

DREAM WEAVER

Kristen watched her dream play out on the huge screen attached to the laboratory wall. She'd expected her dreams to have been about a certain boy, as that's who she spent most of her time awake thinking of. But instead, she was driving a blue Chevrolet around a dusty mountain road, as police vehicles gave chase. A hundred helicopters thrummed in the red sky above, filling it like a murmuration of starlings. Her side window was wide open, her arm stretched out of it, a silver pistol in her hand. She fired three shots into the sky while shouting *"Yippee!"* over and over again.

Professor Danielson laughed as she watched the scene. Kristen's cheeks flushed hot with embarrassment. She didn't even have her license in real life, so it was weird watching herself drive on the open road.

It was such a strange, unnerving experience, letting someone watch your dreams. There was, she suspected, nothing more private than one's own dreams. No safe in the world more secure than your own mind. And yet, Professor Danielson had cracked the safe and was revealing all the secrets she held inside.

"This is wonderful," the professor said, clapping her hands. "Just wonderful. It's like watching a movie."

Not like any movie Kristen had ever seen. The screen was fuzzy with black-and-white lines spearing down it every few seconds like lightning. And usually, movies didn't change scenes so abruptly. In her dream, she drove her car through a mountain tunnel and came out the other end into the murky depths of an ocean. The car was gone, and jellyfish swam around her. No, not swam. They danced.

"I'm sorry, Professor," she said. She wasn't sure what she was sorry for. It wasn't her fault exactly. Professor Danielson knew even better than she did that you couldn't control your dreams.

"Call me *Susan*," she said. The professor had told her to do just that a dozen times since she'd met her yesterday.

Professor Danielson—Susan—studied dreams. The college had recently funded Professor Danielson for her groundbreaking research, but she'd only now reached the stage of needing volunteers for her dream machine. *Paid* volunteers. The paid part being the lure that had caught Kristen when she saw the flyer on the activities board at school.

She'd been the first, and so far the only, volunteer. Kristen had spent last night—her first night as part of this dream team—in a rather remote lab at the rear of the college campus. After handing over the required permission forms, her mom headed home, and Susan had led her to a single medical bed hidden behind a curtain. Then she clamped wires onto her neck, head, and face. Kristen could see the signals sent from her brain pulse on a nearby console as an array of colorful lights.

None of it had hurt. It'd just been a little hard to fall asleep, as she'd had to lie on her back when usually she slept on her side.

Susan had been with her the entire night, taking notes and checking connections. Kristen had woken once or twice to see the professor staring at stacks of numbers on one of the monitors. Susan had turned to her and put a finger to her lips. "Hush. Go back to sleep."

She'd felt safe and warm knowing someone was watching

over her as she slept. But now, in the cold light of early morning, with Susan rubbing her hands gleefully, she just felt awkward. She held a hot cup of coffee in her hands; the steam and the sweet nutty scent were heavy with reality.

"Do you know what we've done, Kristen?" Susan asked.

She shook her head.

"We've proven my theories correct. You're going to be famous. As famous as I am. You're the first person whose dreams have been recorded. That can be watched. Your dreams will be ana- lyzed for decades as I try to make sense of them. They will help me understand the very purpose of dreams."

Kristen had often wondered what dreams meant. When she was younger, she'd had a book that had helped to interpret her dreams and explain what each one meant. But the book's answers were vague and often made things even less clear than before. It wouldn't have been able to tell her what dancing with jellyfish meant—of that she was certain.

She was about to ask Susan why people dreamed at all when the professor's phone rang.

"I'll just be a moment," she said. She heard Susan greet the caller and leave the lab. Kristen sat there alone, legs swinging from her bed.

Her dreams had apparently come to an end. The screen that had been playing them now showed a fuzz of black-and-white dots.

Kristen couldn't help herself; she got up and walked curi- ously to the console. It didn't look hard to use; there were only a handful of buttons. Kristen wanted to watch the car chase again. It might not have been the dream she'd been expecting to have, but it was kind of cool all the same.

She clicked a button that looked like a rewind symbol.

The screen on the wall hazed white, flickered yellow, then began to play.

It took her a moment to realize she hadn't rewound her dream, but rather she'd moved on to someone else's dream.

On the screen, a castle stood on a mountain, illuminated occasionally by lightning, as a storm raged around it. The camera slowly zoomed in. She only knew it was a dream and not a movie because the castle wobbled and changed layout every second or so, as if the dreamer didn't have a firm grip on what it should look like.

The camera panned past a misty graveyard and in through a solid brick wall, then fell down into a dungeon lit only by candlelight.

A body lay writhing and chained to a metal platform. A shiver sailed down Kristen's spine.

A woman with a crooked back and a scalpel in her hand was bent over the unfortunate person.

Kristen wondered, *Whose messed-up dream was this? And why did that body look so familiar?*

If only the woman would move so she could get a better look at the face.

She jumped as the woman turned. As she grinned at the camera.

Her face was deformed: lopsided and almost falling off itself. But she recognized Susan all the same. Those cold blue eyes like a dead and frozen planet.

This must have been one of Susan's dreams. But what was she doing? It seemed like she was performing some sort of experiment on the chained-up girl. Or surgery, maybe.

Now that the professor moved, she got a better view of the girl on the table.

"Oh god," she said, as she recognized the person. The person that looked very much like her.

"Oops," said a voice behind her. "You weren't meant to see that."

Susan was back in the room. A scalpel in her hand.

"What's going on?" Kristen cried.

"What are dreams?" Susan said. "Isn't that the real question?"

"What are *you* is my question," she whimpered.

"Dreams," Susan said, ignoring her, "are simply projections of our innermost desires. Our most protected secrets. I unlocked yours and now they belong to me. And now you've seen mine. In that way, we belong to each other."

She smiled like the devil might have done.

Susan gently closed the door behind her, locking it with a key.

Kristen looked around for another exit, but there weren't any. She suddenly knew this "professor" had no intention of letting her leave. Not alive anyway.

"Please," Kristen said.

"You weren't really the first, I'm afraid. This isn't even the first college I've gathered students from. But I promise you, your dream will be as sacred to me as every other in my collection."

She felt a hot sick rising inside her. Her dream . . . It was going to be a serial killer's souvenir.

"Don't worry," Susan replied, padding slowly toward her, a fiery glint in her eye, twirling the surgical scalpel in her hand.

"Perhaps this is all just a bad dream."

SCAN THE CODE
FOR A SCARE

↓

TOO
SCARED
TO
SLEEP

STAGE FRIGHT

Whenever Ethan got onto a stage to perform, he froze like a snowman. It was the audience, you see: how they looked at him, stared at him with their hard, assessing gazes. They were just waiting for him to slip up, to sing a single faulty note. Then they'd grin with wide, mocking lips.

His parents told him it was all in his head, that it was just stage fright. That getting up in front of so many people would make anyone anxious.

It didn't matter to Ethan whether it was in his head or not. The feelings in his gut and pounding of his heart were absolutely real.

He'd started singing when he was seven, and his parents realized instantly he was something of a prodigy. Everyone knew he was good. Brilliant, even. If he'd just enter one of those singing competitions on television, they all said, people in the industry would discover him and he'd become world famous.

But he couldn't even perform in front of his closest friends without anxiety gnawing at his belly like a wolf.

He'd tried therapy with no success, and more recently hypnosis. Now, whenever he heard a bell ring twice, he'd hop around on one leg. But his stage fright was no better.

At fourteen, Ethan finally found a potential solution online, digging through Reddit threads. The post didn't have much activity, but the website seemed legit.

"I don't know," Mom had said when he showed her the page. "That's pretty expensive."

"He'll earn it back in no time," said Dad, "if it allows him to perform."

Mom had given in eventually, and the next day they'd booked an appointment with an OptiGone specialist.

"Your son's a perfect candidate for the procedure," said Dr. Haletty, a tall lady with short hair and a scar beneath her eye that made Ethan uneasy. Her office building had been a bit nondescript, but he had assumed it was for privacy reasons.

"Is it safe?" Mom asked.

Ethan usually rolled his eyes at his mom worrying. But that scar, bright red, trailing down the doctor's face from beneath her left eye . . . it made him worry, too.

"Perfectly. We have a hundred percent satisfaction rate. We've had no complaints from any customers."

"How does it work?" Dad asked. "We watched the video, but it only showed the results of the procedure, not how it's done."

The doctor smiled. "It's simple, really. Like placing a permanent contact lens over Ethan's eyes. Only these are digital contact lenses changing the information that's transmitted to his brain."

"So I won't see anyone in the audience at all?" Ethan asked, his worry giving way to hope.

"Not if you don't want to. Or, if you prefer, you could choose to see a very limited audience—the first row. The first few rows. Just a sprinkling of people here and there, and the rest of the seats will appear empty."

"How do I control it?" he asked. "How do I change the settings?"

"It takes a little practice," the doctor confessed. "But in essence, you squeeze your eyes shut nice and tight and imagine the audience you want to see. The chip in each lens will latch on to this, and when you open your eyes, how you *imagined* the audience is how you'll see them. Reality will be augmented to help your brain overcome your nerves."

He took a nervous breath. "Okay. Let's do it."

"Are you sure?" Mom asked. "You don't need to, you know. You don't have to be a singer. We'll love you no matter what you choose to do."

"He was born to be a singer," Dad said gruffly.

"I want to," said Ethan.

And that was that.

The doctor nodded. "Lovely. Then let's get you on the schedule."

He was unconscious for the operation. He'd had no choice. The lenses needed to be grafted onto his eyes and the circuit connected to his optic nerves so that the altered images could be sent directly to and from his brain.

The day after the operation, his eyes a little red and a little sore, he'd decided to try out the new lenses. Rusty, the family's old Labrador, had been yapping and jumping around him, begging for a walk. Ethan closed his eyes and imagined the dog gone from the kitchen. Imagined the wooden linoleum bare, except for Ethan.

When he opened his eyes, Rusty was gone. Holy mothballs, it'd worked! Sure, he could still hear Rusty and feel his paws as the dog jumped up against him. But he couldn't see Rusty.

This was going to change everything.

Whatever Ethan wanted to vanish, he could make vanish. No more audience. It was the first step on the ladder that would take him to the very top of the world.

Except try as he might, he couldn't get Rusty to reappear. He closed his eyes and attempted to remember exactly what Rusty looked like, each and every inch of fur, then opened them.

No Rusty.

He stared at a photo of him and Rusty from last year, both sitting at the top of a windy hill. Then he closed his eyes and remembered the scene. Still no Rusty.

Ethan should have told his parents that he couldn't see the dog anymore—but he was worried they'd flip out and make him have the procedure reversed. The lenses worked and that's what mattered. Besides, the procedure *couldn't* be reversed. Not without the risk of losing his vision entirely.

"They work great, Mom," he lied when asked. "I tried them on the dog, and he vanished."

"Well, don't use them on me," she said with a laugh. "I don't want you ignoring your mother." She paused. "Was it easy to bring Rusty back?"

He smiled. "Pretty easy."

Before long, he'd made it to the live final of the biggest talent show on television. During each round, he'd vanished the audience. But this round, knowing that millions at home would be watching, he'd gotten onstage and the music had started, and that old familiar anxiety reared its head.

Ethan stood there trembling, unable to sing. So many people watching. The eyes of the world on him.

He closed his eyes.

He knew he'd regret it. Shouldn't do it. But what else could he do? He imagined that everyone watching him in the audience and at home would disappear.

When he opened them, he sang like a bird freed from its cage.

Later in the evening, a hand grabbed him and led him back onto the stage. He heard voices congratulate him on the huge win and on his incredible performance.

The same voices invited his parents onto the stage with him. Perhaps they were with him now, just next to him.

He didn't know.

Because for Ethan, he was all alone in the vast empty arena. Forever.

SCAN THE CODE
FOR A SCARE
↓

TIME TO GO

The surgery was a success! After they got home, Suzie stood by the sink ready for a trial run. A vast pile of dirty dishes surrounded her. Never in her life had she been excited to do dishes before, but now she was buzzing to start.

She took out her phone and opened the app that linked to the chip in her head. Her palms were sweaty, and her finger smeared the screen. She was excited and a bit nervous. But she'd seen her dad use it a hundred times before—there was no reason to be scared.

Suzie set the app's timer for ten minutes, starting one minute from now. Then she filled the sink with hot, bubbly water and plopped the nearest filthy plate into it.

They were all clean by the time she came back to reality. Suzie found herself drying her hands with a dish towel.

"What the heck happened?" Then she laughed. Holy cow, it'd worked perfectly. She hung the towel up and took out her phone. The ten-minute session was logged right there in the app.

Suzie sort of remembered doing the washing. Sort of. The memory was a bit like watching a movie through thick clouds of fog. Dulled, but just about visible.

For the first time ever, she was excited to go to school.

Suzie hadn't been totally honest with her father about why she'd wanted the SUB chip installed. She'd said it was just to skip the "boring" parts of the day like chores. But that wasn't the truth. Skipping the dishes was a bonus. As was fast-forwarding her walks with Nola, their chocolate Lab, and skipping her homework. But they were not why she'd craved it.

The truth was that her dad was sick. The doctors were hopeful they'd find a cure—and there were promising clinical trials and treatments—but he was in a lot of pain. Suzie knew it wasn't his fault, but seeing him suffer every day was unbearable to watch. She'd already lost one parent to cancer. She couldn't bear to watch another one go the same way.

Dad's treatment took him to lots of different places, so they'd moved around a ton. Which made making new friends annoying. Not that Susie wasn't good at making friends; she was. On top of that, she was a smart kid—good grades came easily to her.

But she was tired of doing it. Starting over time and again. She knew her dad would be okay soon. The doctors at this hospital seemed confident they'd found a cure. Still, knowing the future would be okay didn't make the present any easier.

The chip would.

After months of pestering her father, he'd relented; he signed her up for the clinical trial, signed the parental consent form, and took her to get the surgery on a Saturday morning. In the waiting room before the procedure, Suzie had been positively giddy. She'd looked over and grinned at her father, but he'd just smiled back weakly. He coughed into his hand, and then stared ahead as if deep in thought. He must've turned on his own SUB to wait out her surgery.

Standing in her kitchen now, she wondered how she'd look when the chip—or her subconscious, more accurately—took over. Sometimes Suzie would catch Dad "checked out," as they called it. Late some evenings, he'd sit on the sofa with pictures of Mom lying next to him. And he'd only seem a little bit different, a little slower to react to her questions. Distant.

She guessed that's how she'd look, too. And that was acceptable—it was worth it—because her chip would change everything for her.

Suzie tested the chip more thoroughly during the second week of school. She stayed fully conscious for her classes but activated it to skip lunch—the most awkward time to meet new people. That evening, as she thought back on her day, she vaguely remembered talking to a few kids. She might've been laughing? She couldn't be sure.

The day felt as distant as a dream, like she'd watched it happen to another person.

And just like that, Suzie was hooked.

The next week she skipped an entire school day, even the classes. Why not? She was smart enough to pass the tests and exams, even if she only had a vague recollection of the lessons she'd attended. She'd wake up at seven in the morning, eat breakfast, then activate the chip. Next thing she knew, she was back home chilling on the sofa, school done.

Boom, she thought. *I could get used to this.*

The following week, she skipped three days of school. The week after that, she skipped all five. Suzie felt good about it, too. She was able to enjoy the fun moments—like bingeing new TV shows and scrolling through social feeds—and forget about the boring ones.

It was during that time that her father's cough grew steadily worse. He'd been struggling to do his own chores and to keep up with his job. If she'd just stopped using the chip then, things might have ended differently.

But instead, Suzie started skipping most of the moments she

spent with her father. He was kind of a bummer to be around. The doctors said he might get worse before he got better. As he became weaker, their time together became too tough to handle. Dinners, walks, and talks became doctor visits, treatments, and pill counting. And it was so easy to skip ahead, to not deal with any of it.

It was on a Sunday that Suzie sat in her room, staring into her mirror. She should have been sleeping, but Dad's coughs were so loud that they rattled the walls and windows. Every three minutes he coughed, like a well-timed missile strike. She switched on her music but somehow could still hear Dad's hacking over the bass.

It made her feel ill just to hear.

She took out her phone and opened the SUB app. She idly spun the wheel to select the number of hours, with no real intention to activate it. Twelve hours. Twenty-four. Every time her father coughed she whirled the wheel again. Two days. Four days. Seven days.

How long would it take for his illness to finally improve? A couple of weeks, probably.

Another cough. Another spin. Fourteen days.

There was still a month of school left before spring break. If she was going to skip two complete weeks of her life—which she still had no intention of doing—then it could just as easily be a month, couldn't it?

Cough. Cough. Cough.

It was almost midnight and Suzie was exhausted. She imagined a long, peaceful sleep. A hibernation away from the world.

Thirty days. Thirty days and then Dad would definitely be better. And school would be over.

Her finger wandered idly, perhaps subconsciously, to the Start button.

She clicked.

The haze was thick this time: not a fog that she could squint through, more like she'd been wearing an eye mask that blocked out all memories of the missing month.

She returned to consciousness standing on the drive outside her house. The sky was bright and burned her eyes.

"Are you all right, dear?" came a voice she vaguely recognized.

A tall woman in a black dress stood next to a Honda Civic.

"Aunt Katie?" she asked. What was her aunt doing here? And where was Dad's car?

Her aunt walked over and placed an arm around her, rubbing circles on her back. "I know this is a very difficult day for you. An impossible day. But I'll be here with you for every step of it."

"A difficult day?"

It was only then she realized that she was dressed in black, too. A long, flowing dress that she'd never seen before.

"Where's my dad?" she asked in a whisper.

There was a pause before her aunt replied. "Waiting for us at the front of the church."

"He's . . . dead?" she asked, but she already knew.

It had only been one month. They still had more time. They had to.

"Oh, sweetie, it'll be okay."

Suzie was panting. Hyperventilating. Hot bile rose up her throat; she swallowed hard to force it back down. "I just . . . I just need to get something from the house. I forgot something."

Before her aunt could say a word, she turned and ran inside. She unzipped the black purse she'd been holding and rummaged through it until she found her phone.

The panic set in. He was never supposed to die. The doctors had been so sure. He was going to get better. There was no way she could go to his funeral. No way she could handle any of this. She crumpled onto her bedroom floor, and the tears finally came.

And underneath her grief lurked another feeling. Guilt.

"I'm so sorry, Dad." Had he known she was checked out for his last few weeks on earth? He must have realized. She'd always known when he was checked out.

What she'd give to go back!

But there was no chip or app that could reverse this. The only way left for her was forward.

Perhaps there was even a time, in the far distant future, when she'd come to terms with it?

She had to get out of here. She opened the app and spun the time wheel. The hours became days, became months, became more than months, and she kept on spinning, not looking at the numbers themselves.

As the wheel still spun, she clicked.

Suzie awoke feeling like only a moment had passed. Just a few seconds.

She now lay on a hard bed in a well-lit white room that reeked of antiseptic.

Strange, smiling faces surrounded her. One face was so

silvery it looked more like a robot's than a person's. Above the strangers, party balloons tapped at the ceiling.

A banner in the corner read *Happy Birthday, Grandma!*

What was going on?

Slowly, painfully, she raised an arm. Suzie gasped as she saw her wrinkled, liver-spotted flesh. She tried to sit up, but her body felt weak. It was only then that she noticed an oxygen mask wrapped around her face and an IV taped into her arm.

Oh no, she'd gone too far.

She'd gone far too far.

SCAN THE CODE
FOR A SCARE
⬇

BROTHER

Otto's parents were talking about his dead brother again.

They thought Otto was asleep, but he was listening to them from the top of the stairs.

Otto was only fourteen, but he understood that his parents were trying to re-create his brother. It wouldn't be the exact same brother he'd lost, of course. They'd grow a new body with James's DNA. He would walk, talk, and look like James. He just wouldn't *be* James. Not really.

Most people didn't know this technology existed, but Otto's mom worked at one of the most advanced tech labs in the world.

Dad didn't want a clone son at all, but Mom kept saying it was better than nothing.

Otto hadn't known James. He hadn't even been born yet when his brother had died. He'd only learned what had happened from overhearing his parents talk about it on nights like these.

"The science is better than ever," Mom said. "This is my work, Richard. Trust me. You do trust me, don't you?"

"His brain's gone, Laura. His memories. It's not like it can just be downloaded. All we'd be able to do is show him photos and tell him stories. But he'd be missing everything between the stories. The little moments that make him human."

"No," Mom said. "We can do more now. That's the point. We can fill in all the gaps when we create him." She sighed then added, "You never listen."

"Of course I listen. And I know that you can fill them with

memories from *other* children. Not James's memories."

"But they'll be good memories. Happy ones. And he'll think they were with us."

"It still won't be him, Laura."

"It'll make us happy again." Her voice softened. "A family."

Otto's heart hammered in his chest. Happy *again*. Because they weren't happy now.

He got up and returned to his room, slipping the door shut behind him.

A stray tear escaped down his cheek as he got into bed. He wanted his mom to be happy. For as long as he could remember, his parents had been sad. They'd had him—a second child—to forget about the one they'd lost, but it hadn't worked. He wished he had fond memories of vacations at the beach, or camping, or any of the stuff they'd done with James. But they didn't want to do any of that with him. Perhaps it reminded them of who he wasn't.

Otto wasn't James. He never could be.

The door creaked open, and light sliced into the darkness.

"Hey, bud." His dad flicked on the lamp and sat on a chair by the side of Otto's bed. "I heard your door squeak. Guess we must have woken you up, huh?" Dad looked sad and soft in the pale light.

Otto nodded.

"How much did you hear?"

"Just that Mom wants James back."

Dad nodded slowly and even managed a smile. "It's just, your mom thinks she could make another James. He's the reason for all her work. And I . . . Well, I don't believe a clone is the same thing." He paused. "But you know your mom—she can be very persuasive."

"So I'd have a brother?"

"Sort of. It'd be complicated. But listen, it's nothing for you to worry about. I won't let her do it to you. You understand?"

Otto nodded again. But if there was one thing Otto understood, it was that Mom always got her way.

"Okay, enough talk," Dad said. "It's time for sleep. Sorry for keeping you up." He leaned over and squeezed Otto's shoulder before getting up and leaving the room.

Otto lay in bed and listened to the thrum of cicadas outside the windows. He felt bad for his parents. And for James. And selfishly, he felt bad for himself, too. He could never be loved as much as his dead brother.

Otto imagined the happy life of the brother he never knew: James chasing seagulls on the beach. James's bright smile in the train window. James happy, hanging upside down on the monkey bars.

All those stories they'd told him. He knew James's life better than anyone. Better than he knew himself.

And wasn't that a bit strange?

I won't let her do it to you, Dad had said.

Let her do . . . what?

He got out of bed and silently opened the door. The hallway was dark, but there were lights on downstairs. Good. They hadn't gone to bed yet.

He pushed their bedroom door open. He prayed his parents hadn't heard it.

The bed was made, and the room was tidy. The shelf was lined with photos of his parents and of James. He thought he'd seen them before, but it had been a long time.

He picked up one of the photos—his parents and James sitting on a boulder, the sea raging behind them. Apart from his hair being shorter, he was starting to look a lot like James. Otto's chubby face had become thinner in the last year. It could slip on top of James's now like a jigsaw piece.

Why were his hands trembling?

We can do more now. Fill in the gaps.

It still won't be him, Laura.

Still. What did Dad mean by still?

"I told you not to come in here."

Otto jumped at his mother's voice. "Mom?"

She gently pried the picture from his hand and ran a finger over James's cheek. "You would have liked him. Everyone did. He was perfect."

Dad stood by the door. He glared at his wife.

She continued. "I'm just shocked it took you this long to figure it out."

"Figure out . . . what?" Otto asked, even though he feared he already knew the answer. Sweat beaded on his forehead. Otto's eyes roamed over the photos in the room. Photos of James. He was so very similar to his brother now. Eerily, terrifyingly, similar.

"He knows. But he's pretending not to."

"Laura!" yelled Dad. "No!"

"You were a good attempt," said Mom, smiling sadly, like a doctor delivering bad news.

"Will you stop talking like that!" Dad bellowed. "Acting like he's not even a person!!"

Otto's heart beat in his throat. *His* heart? *His* throat? Were either of them really his?

"I'm him, aren't I?" Otto said. "I'm a . . . clone."

"Told you he knew."

Dad trembled, with rage or terror, Otto wasn't sure. Then

he sighed, and it was as if all the emotion leaked out with the breath. "I'm so sorry, Otto. I didn't want this."

A sinking pit grew in his stomach as Otto realized his entire life was a lie. He needed to think. To be alone.

"I'm going to bed," Otto said. He started toward the bedroom door, but his mom stepped in front of him.

"No." Mom smiled. "You'll join your other failed . . . brothers . . . outside."

"In the barn," said Dad, nodding encouragingly. "It won't be so bad. I even put a flat-screen out there."

Otto looked back and forth between his parents' faces, waiting for one of them to tell him this was all a sick joke. Surely, they weren't serious. "What the heck? This—this is my house. I'm not leaving. You are my family."

"James was our family," said Mom, not meeting his gaze. She shifted her weight impatiently, as though weary of the conversation.

Otto's knees started to quiver, and he thought he might pass out. Instead, he stood up straighter and willed his voice to sound steady. "What am I, then?"

Mom finally looked at him. Her gaze was cold, impassive. "It's always good to have spare parts. For when we have our precious boy back. We lost him once. That won't happen again."

Otto now understood what he truly was. Not a son. Not a boy. Not even a person. He was only spare parts.

"Nooooo!" he screamed. Dad grabbed his arms. Otto fought against him, but it was no use. Dad dragged him toward the door.

"I can do better!" Otto wailed. "I promise!"

His mother sighed. "You all say that. But in the end, it's just not enough."

There you are alone in bed
With swarming thoughts
Inside your head
You think and touch and smell and feel
But have you asked
If you are real?

SCAN THE CODE
FOR A SCARE

↓

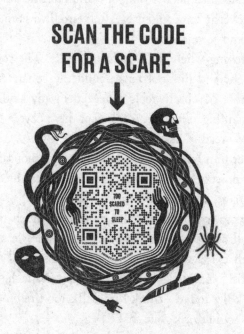

VIRUS HUNTER

My name is Xavier. I used to be someone's son and someone's brother. But now I'm a Virus Hunter. I play games to save lives—I've been doing it for months, maybe years, it's hard to say. All I know is that people count on me.

You see, I won a gaming competition. Got the highest score, made the fewest mistakes. I hadn't known—not back then—that the game had been a sting operation to find an elite gamer that the government could use. Afterward, I was brought to this underground compound.

I'm sleeping when the lieutenant enters. The room's lights flare yellow, and his footsteps pound the concrete. My head pounds, too. My brain feels squeezed by my skull, as if my skull's shrinking. The pain is frequent these days.

"Are you ready?" asks the lieutenant.

I've met him hundreds of times, maybe a thousand by now, but I still don't know his name. He'd been introduced to me as the lieutenant, and that's still all I know.

I sit up in my bunk, no clue as to how much time passed since I fell asleep. Down here, in this windowless basement, time barely exists. Sometimes I feel like I lose days all at once.

"I'm still exhausted," I say. "I have that headache again, and it's a real killer today. I think I might be too tired to game."

"You should drink your shake."

He was, of course, referring to the daily smoothie they provide. I want to respond and say I'm done drinking that crap, that it tastes like expired milk and rust. But I also know that it's the only food I get, twice a day. Besides, it always makes the headache go away faster.

"Lucky for you," he continues. "It looks like it just arrived." He smiles as he hands it to me.

I swallow as I pinch my nose. Disgusting, as usual. But the fog in my head lifts, the pain becomes muted. I can think straight again.

The lieutenant plugs a thick cable into my neck, clicking it into a socket that was installed a long time ago. It stings but not unpleasantly.

"Who're we saving today?" I ask.

"That's need-to-know info. And you don't need to. Not right now."

"Sir, yes, sir," I say mockingly, adding a lazy salute to upset him. It's the little things that get you through a life like this.

He snorts, or it might be a growl.

I never know whose lives I'm saving. Rich people, probably. Maybe politicians. But I always do the job. What choice do I have?

When I was brought here, they explained how the "game" worked. I control a nano ship that's injected into a sick patient. The nano ship is a robotic vessel, no bigger than a millimeter long, which fits snugly into a syringe that sails directly into the patient's bloodstream. I control the ship from the command center, an eight-foot metal tube in the corner of my room that sort of looks like a metal casket. My controls mirror the ship's. My mission—each level—is to eliminate the disease or virus from the patient's body. From the ship's microscopic camera, I see everything it sees and control its weapons. Kill the virus.

....

I've become pretty good at it. None of my patients have ever died; I have a hundred percent success rate. Even still, I get a little nervous when the game begins to load. Every second and every shot matters. With aggressive diseases, there's no going into the patient twice. The stakes of this game are literally life and death for someone.

I miss home. Every day I want to escape. But they told me when I arrived that one of the patients I'd save would be my little sister. A few years ago, she became very ill. She'd been through every treatment available, but she just couldn't get well. The doctors thought she might have a new kind of virus, and that maybe, if they could just keep her alive long enough, they would find a cure. I never suspected that *I* might be the cure.

They wouldn't tell me when I'd be fighting for her. They're clever like that. They knew I'd stay and play the best I could for each patient, just in case it was her I was saving. And they were right.

Maybe I've saved her by now. Or maybe I will today.

I slip into the familiar metal frame and take my place at the command post. The lieutenant slides a flat key into a terminal on the wall. Lights and symbols flicker on a monitor.

The lieutenant flicks a switch. The world fades away, and suddenly I'm pulled through viscous red water.

I become the ship that has been injected into the sick patient. I am now the Virus Hunter.

I've barely oriented myself to the new game world when the virus attacks me. Chunks of spinning darkness hurtle out of nowhere. Their bodies are pocked by red dots like eyes, with rows of razor-sharp pincers on their sides.

They take at least a dozen bullets each before they fall. More than any enemy I've come across before.

I broadcast my voice into the real world and ask, "What the heck are these things?"

More are coming. They're oozing out of the walls, out of the veins and arteries. And the walls themselves no longer look smooth and pink but greenish, with raw, ragged, saucer-shaped holes. I don't know whose body I'm in, but I'm pretty certain it's already screwed. There's no way I can defeat this many creatures.

The lieutenant's voice rings in my head: "It's a new virus. The fact that it even exists is an accident. Do your best and then do better."

They're clinging to my vessel now, their claws snapping against my hull. They'll destroy me soon. There are too many to fight off.

I've never lost a patient before, and I'm thinking of my sister, but this one is beyond hope—or at least beyond my skills. "Get me out," I say. "This is over. Get me out!"

"Negative, Major," says the lieutenant over the comms. "This is a very special patient. One we really don't want to lose."

I'm suddenly nervous. I'm thinking presidents, I'm thinking world leaders and scientists. Who could it be? I suddenly realize it doesn't matter. What would it change? The fact is I can't save them.

Before I have time to puzzle it out, I'm traveling fast, heading into the stomach. It looks like an old sponge, too dirty to even clean a counter. There's something caught in the folds of the stomach wall. It's metal, dull, and oddly shaped. It almost looks like the arcade token I swallowed when I was eight. I can even read the logo through my screen as I go by—wait! *Funky Pin*, it reads.

What are the chances? The name on the token is the very same arcade . . .

"Lieutenant . . ."

I'm finding it harder and harder to concentrate. The pain in my head is back, and I feel like I'm moving in slow motion. "Who is the patient?"

There's only silence on the other end. I need to get out. "Lieutenant, what is going on? Why is there a Funky Pin arcade token in this patient? I'm starting to get freaked out."

No response.

"Do I know this person?" I ask, a little louder. "Pull me out."

No response.

"PULL ME OUT."

My heart feels like it's going to burst through my chest. There's a long-dispirited exhale on the other end of the comms.

"It's you."

Chills crawl up my body like spiders.

"Wha . . . what?"

He answers, "It's you. You're the patient, Xavier."

My grip on the ship's control slackens, and I feel like I might pass out. The ship rocks back and forth as the virus tries to unhinge it.

"Me?"

"The shakes, they were intended to help you in the game. To increase your reaction speed, to keep you awake longer for critical patients. And they did that. They worked very well for their intended purpose—we got what we needed. Unfortunately, they had a rather unexpected side effect."

I think about the headaches. Time seeming to vanish. Oh no . . .

They used me. Treated me like a lab rat to increase performance. And now I'm inside my own body trying to save my own life.

There's a crack as my ship loses a motor. I fire every weapon, but for each creature I kill another two take its place.

I feel my body swaying, vision narrowing. There's no way I can defeat them.

"Either you win and save yourself," says the lieutenant. "Or you lose."

Danger. The message flashes on the front of my screen inside a big red button. I know there are only moments before the game is over and I fail. What happens then?

"There's still a way out, Xavier. You just have to defeat the virus."

"Please," I beg. "Just let me start over and try again."

The warning flashes again.

Danger.

"I'm sorry, Xavier. It's too late."

Then a *crack*, as the hull of the ship gives way.

In blood I move
In blood I treat
I'd like to go home
But this is my street

SCAN THE CODE
FOR A SCARE

FIVE
MINUTES IN
THE FUTURE

....

I know it seems like these next stories are from a future five minutes—or years—away, but that future is already here. These stories are happening all around you. Right here, right now.

REVEEL

Tommy's featureless new face stared back at him from the sun visor mirror. It twitched and pulsed against his skin, as if it were alive. He watched the white silicon of the mask spread over his face and felt it latch on to him like an octopus's suckers. He grinned; his new, perfect smile was dazzling.

The Reveel mask was a birthday present from his parents. Mom hadn't wanted him to get one. "If someone doesn't want to be your friend without a mask, what makes you think they will want to be your friend with one?" she had asked, but that had only increased his pleading. Now, for his birthday, she'd finally bought it for him! Once it finished configuring itself to his face's dimensions, it would change everything.

He was the only kid left at Southern California's elite Archer Day School without a Reveel—a digital mask that projected a filtered and flawless face on top of your own, hiding your skin's imperfections. Those perfect-looking influencers online? It's not just a filter on their phone. It's a filter on their life, knit into the fabric of their skin. Once the advanced synthetic mesh molds and calibrates to the host's face, it's completely unnoticeable.

No one outside Archer and a few other schools knew about Reveel. But the experiment had been going on for a year and was so far a success. At Archer, no one could live without it.

And Tommy? He was mortified by the bumps, red spots,

and tiny pustules that covered his cheeks, getting even redder and more inflamed every time he was embarrassed.

Tommy had come to hate his skin. To despise it. He wanted it so badly to be perfect like everyone else's. He'd cut off a finger if that's what it took. Then maybe his old best friend, Alicia, would notice him again.

Finally, that anxiety was flowing away, swallowed by the soft silicon layer that already flickered with an image of a better Tommy. As if the true Tommy inside him was crawling up to the surface, finally taking control. He wanted the other kids to really know him.

For once, he was excited to be at school.

"See you this afternoon," Mom said as Tommy climbed out of the passenger seat and grabbed his bag. "Love you."

Tommy could feel his face turn bright red, but he still looked perfectly put together in the reflection of his mom's sunglasses. "You too," he said before closing the car door. For the first time in months, his stomach buzzed with excitement rather than anxiety. Alicia had stopped hanging out with him since she'd gotten her Reveel, and school had become as lonely as an island. Whenever Tommy approached other kids, they'd turn and stare at him until he got the message.

Today he strode confidently through the gates and into the silence of the school grounds. Not that the silence meant it was empty; plenty of kids were standing in perfect circles outside the main building. Ten in each group. Always ten. They were deathly quiet—no talking, even among themselves.

Tommy wondered if they stopped talking to each other because he'd come through the gates, or if they'd been quiet beforehand.

It didn't matter. What *did* matter was that he was one of them again. He always felt like he was behind the social curve, a loner. But not this time. Now he was on equal footing. His face was still his, but also handsome, as if God had airbrushed over it.

He could feel the mask integrating with his own skin. It felt like cool lotion flowing over his natural contours and then tightening, smoothing, and perfecting. It was so seamlessly aligned that he could feel only the smallest seam where the mask ended and his neck began. Tommy loved the feel of it, knowing he was becoming a new and better version of himself.

He approached one of the circles. "Hey, guys. I finally got my Reveel. What do you think?"

Silence. He'd been hoping for something more. Anything.

He could hardly identify his classmates. He recognized Liam's backpack, but not his face. Liam used to have an abundance of freckles and round cheeks. Now he stood picture-perfect, his chiseled jawline practically cutting the sun shadowing his face.

But it was his scowl that was the most off-putting. He was known for always smiling, always being in a good mood. Other kids used to make fun of his infectious "hyena laugh." Now he stared at Tommy, saying nothing.

"So, uh, have you seen Alicia?"

Nothing.

He examined each face surrounding him. No Alicia in this group. Just ten perfect faces looking at him. No, not at him— they were looking past him.

"Never mind," he said, pushing his way out and heading toward the next group.

Before the invention of Reveel, school had been alive with the sounds of chatter and laughter. But that drumbeat had first faded to a mosquito buzz, and then to this—to nothing. Only now did Tommy realize how truly strange it was.

He dipped inside a second circle. More perfect faces stared darkly at him. He almost didn't recognize Alicia. Her face had changed so much. She'd always been pretty, even before the masks. Now she was flawless, her skin smooth and slightly tanned. It should have made her prettier . . . but now she was almost indistinguishable from all the other faces around her.

Tommy remembered how they used to skateboard together as kids. They had this little crappy plastic ramp. Once, Alicia fell so hard that it left a little scar above her right eyebrow. They used to laugh about it now and again, before her Reveel smothered the scar and everything else that reminded him of her—the freckles from summers at the pool, the dimples at the corners of her mouth.

"Hey, Ali, long time no see . . ." Tommy began. His palms were sweaty, so he shoved them into the pockets of his khakis.

Alicia stood silent.

"It's me, Ali. Tommy," he tried again. Maybe she didn't recognize him, either. "Want to go skateboarding after school?"

She stared through him. Something in his stomach turned sour.

"Look, I totally get why you didn't want to hang out with me anymore. I didn't even want to hang out with me." He laughed. "But now I'm like you and . . ."

His voice trailed off. She wasn't listening. His heart sank. Maybe his mom was right. If Ali didn't like him without the Reveel, maybe she didn't like him at all. He turned away quickly because even if she might not be able to read the hurt in his face anymore, she could still see the tears that were threatening to form.

That night, he pried off his Reveel, painfully tugging it off his skin. Places where the mask had been suctioned on the tightest blistered and oozed as he peeled it back inch by inch. By the time he got it all the way off, his face felt raw. He looked in the mirror and tried not to scream. It was red and blotchy. Blood trickled down his cheek. He'd never looked so hideous.

Enraged, Tommy threw the mask out. It squirmed in the trash like a fish gasping for air.

Even so, he felt stupid for thinking the Reveel would help Alicia see him differently. If he had to be a social outcast, so be it. He'd rather be unique. Himself. Even if that meant ugly.

The next day, Tommy arrived at school with his face covered in scabs. He had argued with his mom about going at all, but since she was furious about him throwing away his expensive new present, she insisted he go. Tommy ate his lunch alone, waiting for the bell to ring. When it finally did, everyone filed out of the cafeteria in a neat line—everyone except Alicia. Instead, she walked up to Tommy's table and stood perfectly still, perfectly silent, just in front of him.

"Ali?" he said.

Nothing.

He got up and waved a hand in front of her face. "Ali, I don't know why you're being so weird, but it's starting to freak me out."

Then it happened.

Tommy jumped back.

Ali's face had changed. Just for half a second. He'd seen Alicia's old face, her real face—but something terrible had happened to it. Her skin was bloody and peeling, pus-filled and blistered.

Then the Reveel was back in place, and her face was beautiful once more. But that didn't ease his galloping heartbeat.

"Ali? What just happened?"

It had probably been the mask. Ali making it change to prank him or something. Yet it made him think of his own painful skin when he'd removed his mask.

"Ali? Can you hear me?"

What if the Reveel had slipped up and revealed the true face beneath it? Or what if it was Alicia trying to communicate with him the only way she could? Maybe she was trying to tell him that there was something wrong. Something very wrong.

Ali stood there. Her eyes were on his now. Blue and damp and real—not part of the mask.

"If you can hear me, Ali, blink twice. I'm going to take your mask off, okay?"

The mask flickered again. The terrible visage beneath came back momentarily, as if Ali was saying yes. Slowly, she blinked. Once. Twice.

He placed a nervous hand beneath her chin, and his fingers searched for the raised surface of the mask. But the mask was perfectly smooth against her skin. Smoother than his had been. It was like searching for the start of a roll of Scotch tape.

Her face flickered again like an SOS. A warning. A silent scream. She grabbed his arms hard, gripping desperately.

"I'm trying to get it off!" he said. "Just hold still."

Tommy hadn't heard them approach. Hadn't noticed the

circle of students who surrounded them. Not until the other kids started closing in like a noose.

Ali *had* been trying to warn him . . . but not about her mask.

The others grinned in unison, their smiles like switchblades. They pushed him to the ground.

"Please," he begged as their fingers pressed against his neck.

One of them held something in his hands.

His mask.

"No! No, no, no, no, no!" Tommy screamed, thrashing. Three other children pinned his arms and legs down.

In the distance, Ali's face flickered at him one last time. *I'm sorry,* she seemed to say. *You're one of us now.*

"Yes," they crooned in unison, as they pressed the mask over his face. It gripped his cheeks and neck instantly. A calm washed over him as his classmates scattered.

Then Tommy stood up and walked to class.

His teachers thought he was just like every other student.

Handsome, pretty, lovely
All words, but can be so deadly
A quick look at a reflection
Will only show the imperfection
Handsome, pretty, lovely

**SCAN THE CODE
FOR A SCARE**

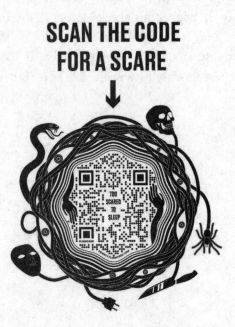

UNBOXED

Chris had a stalker. He was certain of it.

He paused the video playing on his monitor and stared at the brightened frame, his heart pounding. She'd dyed her hair and was dressed in black, but it was her all right. And in her hand, something silver sharply glimmered.

Chris had been editing the latest video he'd intended to upload later for his millions of followers when he'd noticed the figure in the background. In the paused frame, Chris sat at the plastic table in his bedroom with a cardboard box in front of him. It was a typical video—his followers adored his unboxing material. It didn't matter what was inside, whether it was old or new—they only cared about the excitement of the unboxing itself.

But in this frame, outside his own window, there was a girl dressed in black. Almost imperceptible until he'd adjusted the brightness and contrast.

She'd been seen in two other videos he'd uploaded a month ago, both vlogs. The comments section had found her and flooded him with "Who's that girl?" and "There she is again! Did you know she was following you on the train?"

He hadn't known. Not until he read the comments and rewatched the videos.

And now she'd been outside his house with a knife in her hand.

Chris hadn't seen the girl in his videos the last few weeks. Not even his army of eagle-eyed viewers had spotted anything suspicious. He figured that after he'd called the cops and reported her, she'd gotten worried and given up stalking him.

He switched on the camera and sat down at his desk, a bundle of packages in front of him. Today was a live stream. Every week he broadcast one of him opening fan mail live for his followers.

He forced a smile and pretended to be excited. Truthfully, he was exhausted and wasn't in the mood, but he didn't want to seem ungrateful. It wasn't part of his brand.

"Welcome to *Chris Unpacks*, live. And just look what I've got for all of you today. Man, oh man, you've sent in boxes by the dozen. So settle down and get relaxed, and I'll get unboxing for you."

"He looks like he doesn't want to be there," one typed.

Chris saw the comment scroll by and felt a pang of panic. So his followers were starting to notice. He wasn't as good an actor as he thought. It was becoming harder to fake his enthusiasm with each new video.

Chris was sick of opening boxes, but it was the fact that his stalker was back that really had him on edge.

The public didn't care, though. They expected him to keep pumping out content as scheduled, no matter the consequences.

He tore open a thick, padded envelope and took out a packet of Pokémon playing cards. "Well, this was very kind of"—he squinted at the letter that accompanied the cards—"Mike A. Donas to donate these to the channel. Second edition, true collectibles. Very cool!"

It hadn't been his idea to make unboxing videos. That had come from his first subscriber, Cra8tln08, who'd found him on an early upload where he'd reviewed a PC game. Cra8tln08 had commented—his first comment at that time—and said he was a natural, that he was charismatic and handsome.

He'd recorded a dozen other videos after that but struggled to pick up any more subscribers. One day, feeling down about it all, he'd recorded a personal video saying how this was all he'd ever wanted, but he'd failed at it just like he did at everything else—that no one wanted to watch him, so this was going to be his final video.

Cra8tln08 had replied. She suggested he record an unboxing video. Promised him he'd get more subscribers if he did that. Urged him to not give up just yet.

He'd been dubious, but he'd made one all the same. Cra8tln08 had been right; things took off almost immediately. That first unboxing video netted him a dozen subscribers and 3,000 views.

Cra8tln08. He hadn't thought of her in months. She'd been so keen and excited about his videos. Too keen, unfortunately. When he'd become more popular, her loyalty had become something of a problem. She'd spammed his live stream chats and his video comments and would bad-mouth anyone who didn't universally adore Chris's content. Eventually and reluctantly, he'd blocked her.

Chris centered a second package on the table and peeled the tape off the box. Slowly, he opened the flaps.

It was a large box and yet the only thing inside of it was a phone. An odd, old phone. Squared plastic corners, a little frayed, and a tiny screen. Heck, it must have been one of the very first smartphones.

"Well, look at this curiosity from the past," he said to the camera. "Anyone recognize the model?"

No one in the chat did.

Pretty cool—he could get a review video out of this. A phone no one had seen before was something of a novelty. He searched the box for a note to help figure out who'd sent it to him, but there was nothing else inside.

"Whoever sent me this, thank you. But you forgot to include your name, so if you're in the chat right now, let me know."

"Turn the phone on," someone in the chat typed.

Another said, "Yeah, let's see what operating system it uses."

He hesitated. It might spoil the upcoming review video a little. But he was curious, too. Probably as curious as his followers. He held down the button on the corner. "It probably doesn't have any charge right now, so—"

The screen lit up a deep, dark purple.

"Huh. Guess it does."

A minute or so passed before the phone's system loaded up and . . . weird. There were only two apps installed: Gallery and Camera.

"Open them!" the chat room spammed.

He shrugged and clicked Gallery.

Chris's hand began to tremble.

All the thumbnails . . . "Oh Jesus."

Every photo—and there were at least a hundred—was of Chris. Some taken through his bedroom window. One was of him asleep in his bed.

His heart stopped beating for a second. He knew instantly who had taken them. *Her.*

At the very bottom of the gallery was a single video, the thumbnail black. Ignoring the chat, he put on his headphones and clicked Play.

A figure swirled in the darkness.

"I gave you everything you wanted, Chris. And then you banished me. You think it's that easy? You owe me everything! You owe me your life."

The voice frothed with hatred.

He knew instantly who it was, although he'd never heard her talk before.

Cra8tln08.

"You're going to give me everything."

The video ended.

"Sorry," he said to the camera. Whispered to his thousands of followers watching him live. "I've got to go. I'm not feeling well."

The chat was ignoring him. They were spamming a request again. Repeating the same comment over and over:

"Show us the video!"

A deep urge inside him told him to run.

He hadn't heard his bedroom door creak open—the headphones must have dampened the sound. But Chris swiveled his chair just in time to see the girl dressed in black charging at him.

And in her hand, something silver sharply glimmered.

SCAN THE CODE
FOR A SCARE

ALMOST ALIVE

Rory wasn't sure how he stumbled his way into this, but here he was hanging out with the three coolest guys at his school. Eleventh graders. Not just that: eleventh graders who wanted to come over and hang out with a ninth grader.

Rory spent the entire walk home trying to act like he was the most mature fifteen-year-old to ever grace the earth.

"Dude, it's going to be so chill. You'll see," Rory insisted as they walked up his front steps. "We've got a VR set and a hot tub, and my dad just upgraded the flat-screen to HD."

"As long as you have the new DreamCube," Zach said, "we'll be cool."

His buddies, Landon and Aman, nodded and exchanged a low chuckle.

"Oh, we'll be cool, then," Rory said, and instantly regretted it when he saw the scoffing eye roll from Landon.

"Do you really have the new *Sentry Wars*, too?" Aman said.

Rory was grateful Aman didn't point out the dorkiness of what he'd just said. "Yeah, I told you. My dad works with the dev team."

His dad really just designed the in-game textures and weapons, but saying "dev team" made the older boys' eyes light up, impressed.

Rory couldn't help but puff up with pride as he led them upstairs to his room. He threw open the door and declared, "Here it is!"

He expected them to stare at the new flat-screen in

amazement. But they didn't seem to notice the giant TV or the sleek DreamCube on the shelf beside it.

Instead they started coyote cackling and pointing at Rory's bookshelves full of VirtuPets: bears and puppies and cats and lions and elephants. Every color and kind crowded his shelves.

His very favorite, a bright yellow parakeet named Gustav, sat on his bedside table, where he greeted Rory every morning with a robotic and peppy, "Hello there, best friend! It's time to wake up!"

"Sorry," Landon said, "are you still eight years old, dude?"

"Legit." Zach pulled his smartphone from his pocket to take pictures. "I feel like I just stepped back in time."

"Do you actually play with those?" Aman said through his laughter.

Shame burned hot on Rory's cheeks as he stared around the room. He had dozens of VirtuPets, and each one of them had a name and a story. The adaptable AI in their processing units meant that they could do anything a real pet could do: learn their new name, learn tricks, learn to recognize when Rory just needed someone to come over and snuggle him into feeling better.

They were marketed as pets that were almost alive. Almost. Now those black plastic eyes seemed to be mocking him as they reflected back the faces of the older boys hysterically laughing.

Rory swallowed his shame and managed to say in a soft and squeaky voice, "Let's just play."

They all played for a bit, but Rory couldn't shake that horrible feeling of being laughed at. He didn't even care when the guys told him they had a great time and wanted to come over again soon to play more of the game. When they were finally gone, Rory stormed downstairs and grabbed a cardboard box out of the kitchen recycling.

He went back to his room, collected every VirtuPet, and threw them into the box. Embarrassment chewed at his belly as he gathered them up. How had he been so stupid not to throw these out years ago? Or at least hide them?

Rory turned at last to Gustav and hesitated. His bookshelves looked so yawningly empty now. He plucked up the parakeet and smoothed his thumb over the plastic shell of its face. Gustav had been his first VirtuPet, and he always seemed the smartest. He could talk to Rory. Listen. Understand.

"I'm sorry," he said, "but I can't be a little kid anymore."

Rory threw him into the box along with the rest.

He put the box in the back seat of his mother's car. It was only then that hot tears stung his cheeks.

After a couple of weeks, Rory almost forgot about his abandoned toys. But they did not forget about him.

It was the weekend of his parents' anniversary. Rory had convinced them he was old enough to spend just one night home alone. They asked if he wanted to invite a friend to sleep over and Rory scoffed, "Nah, it'll be more fun to stay home by myself." He did not tell them that he didn't have another friend he could invite over. And it *was* fun: staying up as late as he wanted, eating whatever he wanted, watching whatever he wanted.

He told himself this was how Zach and all those older boys felt. Powerful. Invincible. Cool. They really didn't care about anything and didn't need anyone.

But now it was 1:30 a.m. Dark shadows stretched along the walls as he sat alone in the living room, awash in blue light, watching television far later than his parents would have ever let him.

Rory pushed half-melted ice cream around his bowl with a spoon. He was about to shut off the TV and go to bed when he heard it.

A *crunch-crunch* across the gravel on their front walk. Like a neighborhood cat stalking prey through the dark.

Rory picked up the remote and turned down the volume. He tilted his head toward the front door and listened.

As if it knew he was listening, the crunching stopped.

Rory stood to get his phone off the charger, but a noise made him freeze. Nails squealed along the glass of the front door.

Rory flattened himself against the sofa, his mind racing. He could army-crawl across the floor and get to his phone, call the police—or call his mom. Then she wouldn't let him stay home alone again until he was old enough to drink.

Maybe it was just a stray cat. Or the wind. His own imagination.

The piercing, spine-tingling scraping sound happened again.

No. That was real.

Rory's heart lunged for his throat. He did not feel old enough for any of this.

He peered over the edge of the sofa, just enough to look for a shape in the window. But no one was there. Or maybe the intruder was smart enough to press themselves against the door, where they could not be seen.

A tinny, robotic voice called through the door, "Hello there, best friend! It's time to wake up!"

Confusion mixed with the fear. That little voice was unmistakable.

"Gustav?" he whispered.

Rory bolted off the couch and over to the door. And now he saw it, there on the ground: the dark silhouette of the tiny robot parakeet, sitting on the stoop.

Rory eased the door open and poked his head out. He blinked away a rush of confused tears. "Gustav? What are you doing here?"

The parakeet's head swiveled toward him with a mechanical whine. It was filthy, stained with mud and muck, as if it had crawled here from a grave.

"You left us, Rory. All of us." Its plastic LED eyes narrowed into angry slits.

Rory's eyes lifted past Gustav and out across his lawn. Dozens of little dark shapes dragged themselves across the grass. As one, their eyes lit up. A hundred pins of light in the darkness. All staring at him.

Rory shrieked as he staggered backward.

Gustav lunged for him, its robot wings flapping urgently. Its plastic beak hinged open and nipped at Rory's ear. Its clawed feet hooked into the fabric of his T-shirt, drawing lines of blood from his shoulder.

Rory ripped the robot pet off his shirt and threw it across the lawn. He slammed the door shut just as the first wave of robotic infantry reached his front walk.

Gustav just kept click-clicking his beak against the glass.

"Let us in, best friend. We missed you so much."

Rory pressed himself against the door and stared past the living room, through the open walkway of the kitchen, to the glass doors leading out to the patio.

More of his old VirtuPets gathered there, standing up on their hind legs. Scruffy cats and mud-stained dogs. The elephant even carried a pocketknife in the curl of its trunk. They had crawled so far to get here that the soft fur on their robotic paws had worn away to reveal the plastic and metal underneath. Their eyes burned red as their metal limbs shrieked across the glass, hungry for him.

Blood dripped down Rory's ear, grounding him. He ran for his phone and dialed his mother's number. Part of him knew he should call the police, but what would he say? "My old robot toys are attacking me, Officer"?

The phone rang and rang.

Rory shrank himself down and pressed his back against the kitchen counter. From here he could see both the front and patio doors at once.

The VirtuPets were crowding around the front door now. The lower half of the glass was just a wall of red eyes, climbing one atop the other, pressing against the window.

"Pick up," Rory hissed under his breath as the phone rang. "Pick up."

A dull crack resounded through the house. Then a splintering crash as the front window shattered, and the VirtuPets poured in.

Rory snapped his head toward the front door just as an automated voice told him, "You have reached the voice mail box of . . ."

The phone slipped from his fingers.

"Now," Gustav chirped, cheerily, as he led the charge of abandoned toys, "you'll never grow up without us. We'll make sure of it."

Rory screamed and ran, but he wasn't quick enough.

The next day his parents found him surrounded by his VirtuPets: all of them almost alive. Almost.

To be real cool
Sometimes you must be cruel
To yourself and others
But that is the way
We all must play
To be real cool

SCAN THE CODE
FOR A SCARE

HOLO GIRL

Naomi liked facts. She was good with those.

Fact: The last time she saw Elaine, her best friend, Elaine had grinned and said, "See you tomorrow!" That was twenty-four days ago. Naomi had sent forty-seven messages between now and then, and Elaine had only answered with silence.

Fact: Elaine, like any respectable fourteen-year-old, spent every moment of the day glued to her phone. She had to have seen them.

Fact: Elaine had never ignored her before.

Naomi stood in her bedroom, frowning at her phone. The floor-to-ceiling LCD TVs surrounding her depicted the perfect blue underside of an ocean. It should have been calming, but the blue light flickering across her face just drew her anxiety to an even sharper point.

She still remembered the first time Elaine came over. She had gaped at the massive paper-thin televisions and said, "Holy crap, that is too cool!" They'd sprawled on the beanbags for hours, flicking through video search results, gossiping about the time Bella Parsons got gum stuck up her nose. Naomi had so many memories of living vicariously through Elaine, she couldn't remember where her memories stopped and Elaine's began.

Naomi's thumb hovered over the Send button as she read the same message she sent day after day:

Hey girl—it's been a hot minute ;) Where've you been? I
miss you! Let's hang out—Naomi

The same message repeated dozens of times. All of them
had that little message-read check mark below them.

Naomi chewed her lip. She liked facts, and she liked routine.
She had never broken the routine before. Bad Things happened
when she broke the routine because the routine meant rules,
and the rules were simple:

1. Wait for Elaine.
2. Message Elaine at 10 a.m. and 6 p.m. every day, without
   fail, until she reappears.
3. Be the best friend you can be.

But the rules did not tell her how to deal with twenty-four
days of silence.

Fact: Any good best friend would have gone out to find her
by now.

Outside her bedroom window, the sky bled orange into sun-
set. There were another 11.5 seconds left until 6:01.

Naomi's stomach knotted and unknotted. There was that
Feeling. That screaming in every neuron and nerve ending
to obey the rules: message Elaine, message Elaine, message-
ElainemessageElaine.

And for the first time she could remember, Naomi ignored
it. She shoved her phone into her pocket and slung her backpack
over her shoulder. She had packed extra clothes, a water bottle, her pocket-size holo-dog port in case she got lonely on the
walk. Elaine liked the holo dog, anyway. She always marveled
that it could frolic in the lake without getting wet.

Naomi crept downstairs, holding her breath. She hoped her
parents wouldn't catch her breaking the rules.

But downstairs was dark and cold. Usually, when Elaine

was here, the house was alive with light. The sprawling screens would gleam, and her parents would be laughing in the kitchen, sipping wine while their robot maid whipped up whatever dinner Elaine demanded.

She frowned and looked around, unease crawling under her skin. Naomi could not remember the last time she ventured down here without Elaine. Couldn't remember anything from these last twenty-four days but sitting in her room, staring at her phone alone. Waiting.

Naomi tiptoed from the stairs past the living room and froze when she caught sight of them out of the corner of her eye: two shapes in the dark, sitting on the couch. But they didn't move. They didn't even seem to breathe.

Naomi took a step closer and squinted in the gathering dim. Their eyes were open but unseeing. They stared ahead, blankly, like robots with their battery packs ripped out. They looked like her parents . . . only she was certain they weren't.

The anxiety in her stomach threatened to boil into full-on panic.

Fact: Everything was good with Elaine here. Everything was normal. She had to get Elaine back.

Naomi marched to the door and wrenched it open with a trembling hand. She wasn't certain where to go, exactly. She had never been to Elaine's house. Never even left her house without Elaine coming to get her. Another Bad Thing.

If she found Elaine, it would all be worth it. It had to be.

Naomi retrieved the holo dog from her backpack and flicked the projection button on the side. A border collie sprang out in a beam of light, but he looked solid and real as anything. He paced in a happy circle and panted, beaming a doggish smile up at Naomi. His name was Charlie because that was what Elaine always called him.

"Ready to find our best friend, Charlie?" she said, ruffling him behind the ears.

Together, Naomi and Charlie hurried down the street, although the dog didn't seem to have any awareness of her mounting unease. Her blood buzzed hot in her ears as she tried to look normal. Unworried. If Elaine was here, she would laugh her perfect, easy laugh and chide her for being anxious. "Don't be a weirdo."

The sky curled over them like a rotten orange peel, darkening into night. Her neighborhood scrolled past as she walked. For a flickering second the houses looked . . . off. As if they were flat, rolling images that only appeared three-dimensional when she stood beside them. An optical illusion. A trick.

But when Naomi blinked fast, the houses were as normal and whole and real as she was. Still, every window on the street was dark, row after row of empty eyes, staring at her. Even the streetlights were snuffed out, and night was falling like someone had dropped it upon her.

Charlie started to whine.

Naomi quickened her pace, trying to remember the way out of her neighborhood. But whenever Elaine wanted to go to the beach or the mall, she just went. There one second, gone the next, the journey itself clipped from her mind like the scraggly bits of a sheet of notebook paper.

Charlie padded ahead of her and, for a half second, glitched. His body flickered in a pulse of dead pixels, just a dog-shaped error in the universe.

Naomi was digging in her bag for the holo dog's device when she smacked into something solid. Something huge and cold as a wall sprung up out of the sidewalk. She staggered back and gasped, clutching her sore cheek.

But there was nothing in front of her. Nothing but air. Beyond her, the city waited, but it was just a blur of half-formed polygons.

Charlie kept happily trotting along without her.

"Charlie!" she called. "Charlie!"

But the dog left her, just like Elaine had.

There were no rules for this. No routines.

Naomi banged her fists against the wall of empty air in a blind panic. She tilted her head back and saw a thin distortion of a bubble, stretching up over her. Catching her in a glass dome, like the inside of a snow globe.

She wasn't sure when she stopped yelling "Charlie!" and started yelling "Elaine!" but her own voice echoed back to her like a stranger's, thick and choked with panicked tears.

Fact: When you break the rules, Bad Things happen.

Naomi wrenched the phone out of her pocket and went back to the messaging app. Elaine's profile was still open—and there was her best friend's perfect smile. She copied the message and sent it, over and over, because she had no idea what else to say.

Hey girl—it's been a hot minute ;) Where've you been? I
miss you! Let's hang out—Naomi
Hey girl—
Hey—
Hey—

Somewhere, on a side of reality Naomi had never seen, Elaine sat at her desk in her own bedroom, a VR headset wedged firmly into place. It was 6:05 p.m., and the world was still full of light and the buildings did not flatten and disappear when you moved away from them. She was deep into a game with her friends when her phone started buzzing madly. Desperately.

Elaine tilted up the VR headset to glance at it. Her visor flashed red as an enemy team member plasma-beamed her character to death.

Elaine scowled at her phone. There was the same notification, again and again:

(AugReal Friends App): Naomi wants to talk to you

(AugReal Friends App): Naomi wants to talk to you

(AugReal Friends App): Naomi wants to talk to you

(AugReal Friends App): Naomi wants to talk to you

Elaine didn't have time for this. She long-pressed on the app icon until the Delete option appeared, and she tapped it.

"What the heck, Elaine?" one of her friends crackled over the headset. "What was that about?"

"Nothing," she muttered. "Just some stupid app glitching."

White light flashed behind Naomi. She turned, grinning, and saw Elaine there for half a second. Elaine sitting on empty air, a VR headset pushed up on her forehead. Elaine glaring at her phone.

Naomi reached for her as relief surged through her belly.

Then, as suddenly as Elaine appeared, she vanished. There was only a hovering black hole where she had once stood. The color of a glitch: purple-green pixels and infinite dark nothingness.

Fact: There were no rules to save her now.

Naomi opened her mouth to scream but was sucked into the black hole, dissolving pixel by pixel.

SCAN THE CODE
FOR A SCARE

↓

BE CAREFUL
WHO YOU
TRUST

....

BE CAREFUL WHO YOU TRUST
These next stories tell the tales of those who trusted too
willingly. They took for granted that most people in the
world are good and forgot that some are very, very bad.
Let these stories be a warning: Be Careful Who You Trust.

CHAMBER OF HORRORS

"Only one of you will make it out of here alive," came a voice from the speaker in the ceiling.

Clara shivered. The voice sounded inhuman, as if it had been put through distortion software. That certainly added to the horror vibe of this escape room. As if being surrounded by dismembered heads shoved onto spears wasn't bad enough.

But her friends didn't seem as unsettled as she was. Matt and Oliver looked at each other, then laughed.

"Wasn't expecting the voice acting," said Oliver, cocking a grin. "This place is actually kind of cool considering its for extra credit."

"Who would have thought," Matt chimed in, "that getting suspended for not showing up to Ms. Weem's history class would result in something that's actually fun?"

"History's always fun," said Clara. She meant it, as cheesy as it sounded. She'd always loved studying different eras. It made her feel like she was part of something bigger in a weird way. She had a particular fascination with medieval times—especially the gorier details. Their brutal way of life felt so different from her simple suburban existence.

This escape room was a re-creation of a medieval torture chamber. But it was much more than just a couple of phony-looking heads on spikes. A body lying across a table that had been chopped in quarters. A guillotine with a basket of heads in front of it. An opened iron maiden showing its innards of huge spikes, just waiting for a body to swallow. Clara rushed over to the iron maiden. She'd read all about them but had never seen one in person. The spikes looked razor-sharp. She imagined what it might be like to be trapped inside for hours. Or worse, killed.

Everything in here looked so authentic and lifelike. Clara shivered. She couldn't tell if it was with excitement or fear.

"Hey, where's Laura?" Matt asked.

"She must have gone to the bathroom," said Clara. "No big deal. We'll wait for her."

The voice over the speakers came again. This time the distortion software cracked and glitched as she spoke. "She's already with you, Clara."

The three exchanged searching looks. The voice sounded eerily familiar.

"Uh, how does the voice-over woman know your name, Clara?" Oliver asked. "You give it to her when you were booking this place?"

Clara shook her head, a little uneasy. "There was no need to book. This escape room isn't exactly popular. I just called the number on the flyer Ms. Weem gave us. The person on the phone said it was walk-in only."

"Then how does that woman know your name?" Oliver persisted.

"Probably heard you two idiots saying it," Clara said. Oliver pursed his lips at her in mock annoyance, but Clara knew he didn't mean it. Matt was here because he'd been suspended and needed the extra credit. But she and Oliver didn't. They both were getting an A in the class. She was pretty sure the only reason he came was that he knew *she* would be there. A few weeks ago, he had walked her home after Chess Club and looked like he was about to kiss her. But then he'd quickly said bye, and they hadn't talked about it since.

"Riiiiight," Matt said. "She's probably listening in right now." He looked up at the ceiling cautiously, trying to find a camera. "Hey, weirdo!" he called out. "It's rude to eavesdrop, don't you know?"

Clara screamed when she saw the head. It had been covered in wax and shone under the light. It looked all too real.

"What?" Oliver asked. Then he, too, saw Laura's head, a spike running up into her neck.

"Oh my god," said Matt. "Mygodmygodmygod!"

"Relax guys, it's not real," said Oliver, walking over to the head. "It's just a prank. That's how the creepy lady knew your name, Clara. She and Laura are clearly in on this together. They must have made a waxwork of her head. But come on, it barely even looks like her. And you two fell for it hook, line, and—"

He lifted the head from the spike, and something slopped onto his shoes. He stared straight ahead behind his tortoise-shell frames, as though afraid to look down. That's when Clara noticed that the crimson headband she'd lent to Laura was still tightly wrapped around her hair.

It was real.

Oliver vomited as the head rolled across the floor.

"Let us out!" Matt shouted, slamming his fists against the door. A door that had seemed innocuous only moments ago but now felt like a prison gate.

The voice came again. "Only one of you will make it out alive. If you refuse to kill each other, in ten minutes you *all* die."

"What the heck is wrong with you?" Matt screamed. "You're sick!"

"We're all going to die," Oliver said, staring at Laura's head. Her eyes seemed to be looking back at him.

"We're not going to die," said Clara, trying to stay calm. Her mind was racing; it felt like someone had given her ten cups of coffee. "This is just a prank, that's all. An extremely gross prank."

"Clara," said Oliver. "Laura is dead. This is happening."

Clara looked around wildly like a caged animal. "Why are you doing this?" she asked, looking up at the ceiling. "What did we do to you?"

"You wanted to learn history, Clara," the voice said. "How people used to die. How tough life used to be. Well, now you get to *live* it."

Matt walked up to Clara and grabbed her shoulders. "I'm not doing this, Clara. There's no way I'd ever hurt you. I say we wait and see what happens. 'Cause maybe you're right, maybe he is—"

The spike split Matt's neck like a skewer through raw meat. He gurgled a word that Clara couldn't make out, then slid off the spear and onto the floor.

Oliver stood behind him, holding the same spear that not long ago had held Laura's head. He was panting and his eyes were wide. "I'm sorry, Clara. Really. I like you. But there's no way I'm dying today."

Matt's body lay twitching between them.

Clara blinked back tears. There was no time to panic. There wasn't even time to breathe. "Please, Olly. Wait. This is ridiculous. We don't even know what this person wants. I'm sure we don't have to *kill* each other."

Oliver thrust the spear forward; Clara jumped back, but the tip ripped her shirt and grazed her skin. She sucked in a breath at the pain.

"I'm not taking that kind of chance."

Clara's eyes darted over the floor. There had to be something she could use.

The spear tore into her left side just above her hip. She screamed as the pain spread like fire across her.

"I'm so sorry," said Oliver. "Really. But I have to go to college, and win State for Chess Club, and travel the world. There's so much I want to do. I can't die in a torture chamber."

Clara fell to the floor clutching her side. "And I can?"

Oliver stepped toward her and held the spear above her neck. "When I get out of here, I'll send the police. They'll find this psycho."

Clara's eyes were blurred, but she saw something behind Oliver. If she could just get him to move a little to his right . . .

"But, Olly, I . . ." she began. "I *love* you. I've had a crush on you for a long time."

Oliver frowned. "You have?"

"Kiss me," she said, turning and getting up onto her knees. "Before you kill me. Just . . . just one kiss."

Oliver paused. He took a step to his side, then leaned down.

Clara didn't think. She pounced like a leopard, pushing with all her weight against Oliver's chest. The iron maiden lay waiting behind him like a standing coffin. Oliver stumbled back, then fell into the maiden's hollow innards.

Oliver screamed as the spikes tore into his back. Clara was already up, her hands on the maiden's door.

"Go to HELL," she yelled, slamming the iron maiden shut.

Oliver's screams only lasted a second. Then his blood pooled out the bottom.

Clara sat on the floor, holding her wound. She sobbed uncontrollably for seconds or minutes—she couldn't be quite sure. Time had no meaning. Nothing mattered anymore.

"Congratulations," came the familiar voice. It almost sounded like her history teacher, Ms. Weem. Almost. "I knew you'd be the one to make it, Clara."

The door swung open. Clara got to her feet and stumbled out of the chamber.

SCAN THE CODE
FOR A SCARE

A MATCHED SET

These woods had already killed Cole's grandmother, but they still looked hungry.

Cole stood beside his uncle Baxter, back behind his grandmother's cabin. The earth beneath their feet looked a little darker than the rest, like it had been forever stained. Like the soil still held the memory of their grandmother's blood, soaking out of her.

"Is this where you found her?" Cole's dad murmured.

Uncle Baxter nodded. The brothers were twins, but they couldn't be more different. According to his dad, Baxter's slight frame and baby face hadn't changed since they were five. Cole's dad, on the other hand, was broad-shouldered, and his Carhartt jacket was always flecked in dry mud.

In arguments, Baxter always shut down. His father always let his emotions rip.

"I told her it wasn't right for a woman her age, living out here alone like this. Wasn't safe." Cole's dad hooked an arm around Uncle Baxter's shoulders.

"You did everything you could."

Baxter glared at the tree line. His hands clenched and unclenched at his sides.

Cole's grandmother's property, eighty acres of pristine woodland deep in western Montana, bordered a national park. She had cleared half an acre for her little log cabin, her woodshed, the garage, the workshop.

Three weeks ago, Baxter showed up here and found Cole's grandmother dead in her own yard. Cole's family got the full story from the police report. Her body had been out in the elements for days, scavenged, swollen. But one line had horrified Cole as much as it confounded him.

The victim's skin was entirely missing, even between her fingers and toes.

Cole couldn't imagine driving up and finding that.

"It's not your fault," Cole's dad continued. "It's not anyone's fault."

Of course, he had to say that. He had been 3,000 miles away when it happened. He'd fled Big Sky Country as soon as he turned sixteen. Only Uncle Baxter stayed. Only Uncle Baxter checked up on Nana. Only Uncle Baxter really belonged out here.

"It's her fault for being too stubborn," Baxter muttered. There was real frustration on his face.

Cole opened and closed his mouth, not sure what to say. He felt wildly out of place, like he was intruding. He decided to just keep quiet.

Cole's dad patted his brother's arm. "Let's get inside and see how everything looks."

They grabbed their things from the rental car, then went inside. Grandma's cabin had barely changed since the last time Cole had been here a few Christmases ago. There were the dusty cross-stitch samplers on the wall, his grandmother's shotgun by the door, his grandfather's whittled duck collection on every shelf.

But there was something new, too.

There, in the squat single room that served as both the

kitchen and living room, sat a leather couch. It was angular, handmade. The leather was patchwork, joined with random curving lines of stitches. The sofa arms were polished wood, the legs ivory, almost like bone. Baxter had thrown one of their grandmother's old crochet quilts over the back.

Cole pointed at it, questioningly. "Where's the old pullout?"

Baxter looked over his shoulder. His face split with a reminiscent smile. "I made this. I sell furniture now. Custom stuff."

"Oh. It looks pretty . . . professional."

It looked anything but professional, but Cole didn't say that. Instead, he sat down uncomfortably on the rough leather.

"What is this?" he asked. "Deer?"

"Some of it," Baxter called back. "A lot of it is antique. I skinned some of it when I was still in high school."

Cole tried to smile and couldn't. He'd never had the stomach for hunting. His dad's eyes lit up the first time he'd showed Cole how to gut a deer. Cole just threw up in a raspberry bush.

"Hey, Cole, your dad and I are going to go on a walk around the property. Be back soon!" Baxter called. Cole just bobbed his head and pulled out his phone. He didn't have service out here, but at least he had a few games downloaded.

They were gone for a long time. So long, his cell phone battery died. Eventually, Cole got hungry and ate some canned beans and pan-heated hot dogs.

Something crackled and popped. He couldn't tell if it was the wood fireplace in the corner or someone walking outside. Cole startled and looked at his muted reflection in the window. The sun had nearly set.

Where were they?

Eventually, Cole's eyes started to droop, so he pulled his

grandmother's crochet blanket over his shoulders and tried to sleep. But the couch was too small. He tossed and turned for hours, trying to get comfortable.

At some point, he heard the front door to the cabin open and close. His dad and uncle must've come back.

He rolled to stare at the back of the sofa in the low orange stove light. For a long few seconds, he just stared, frowning. He tried to wipe off the leather, but it didn't change.

Adrenaline plucked hot in Cole's veins. He had never felt so instantly awake.

There was a narrow, long strip of leather, sewn into the center couch cushion. It had a distinct smudge, shaped like South America. The smudge was darker than the rest of the leather, but once Cole placed it, it was unmistakable.

That was the port-wine birthmark on his grandmother's upper arm. She used to tap the side of it, jokingly, and tell him it was a sign from God she'd get to retire somewhere tropical one day. She'd never made it farther south than Utah.

Cole's mind flashed back to that line in the police report.

The victim's skin appears to be entirely missing, even between her fingers and toes.

Terror sent Cole rocketing back, off the couch.

He froze in the dark, not daring to breathe. His mind spun, connecting dots that shouldn't have existed, but there they were.

Uncle Baxter had made this couch. Baxter used his own mother's skin as leather. Baxter was a murderer.

He felt like a rat trapped in a box.

Cole took a tentative step. The floorboard beneath him squealed. His pulse hammered so loudly, he was sure Uncle Baxter would hear it. He froze, wincing, until the silence satisfied him. He tiptoed to the table, but his phone was still dead. He searched for car keys but couldn't find any. The shotgun that had been by the door was gone, too.

His stare flicked from the bedroom curtain to the couch. All that leather couldn't come from one body, even if he had taken all the skin. How many people had he killed?

"This can't be happening," Cole whispered, because he needed something in this room to feel real.

A hunting knife sat on the kitchen table. Cole snatched it up. The hilt was cold between his fingers, colder still as he stuffed it into the back of his jeans. He turned, and his gut plunged for the cabin floor.

Baxter stood there, shirtless, bed-headed, and aiming a shotgun right at Cole's chest. He yawned. "This couldn't have all waited until the morning, buddy?"

Cole stepped back until he nearly fell into the fireplace. His heel clattered loudly against the fire poker. He started sidestepping toward the window, but Baxter clucked his tongue and shook his head.

"That's all right. You'd better stay right where you are."

Fury twisted Cole's face. "Did you do something to her? And where's Dad?" he demanded.

"Give me the knife," Baxter said.

"I think you know I'm not doing that."

His uncle just sighed, like they were kids arguing over video games. "I really did want to do this in the morning."

Cole lifted his heel to rest it on the fire poker. He coiled, every muscle screaming at him to run. But he just tossed the knife with one hand and tensed, waiting.

Baxter leaned down, using the nose of the shotgun to nudge

the knife closer to himself. For a split second, he showed the top of his skull, the start of a bald patch.

Cole dropped down, seized the fire poker, and swung the metal rod at Baxter's head like a baseball bat. It connected with the hollow crack of metal on bone, so hard the shock rattled up Cole's forearms.

His uncle collapsed, limp. Blood already bloomed from the back of his skull. Even now, Cole had the insane instinct to see if he was okay. But he stooped, grabbed the knife, and bolted for the door. He would have taken the shotgun, but Baxter had fallen on top of it.

Cole kicked open the cabin door and tumbled down the porch, then ran down the dirt driveway. He whipped his head around for a split second, thinking. He could hide in the woods, but running blindly into the dark could get him lost deep in national park territory. With no supplies, not even a coat, that was just a slower death. He charged for the tree line and—

Something hit him like a kick in the back. He whirled, expecting to see Baxter behind him. But there was no one there. Heat dripped down Cole's back.

A second later, the crack of the shotgun reached his ears.

Cole swooned and staggered, but he stayed on his feet. Through blurring vision, he saw his uncle lurch through the doorway, blood dripping down his face. The shotgun in his hand was still smoking.

"That wasn't even a good hunt," Baxter said.

Cole took one step, then another, then collapsed to his knees. He looked down to find an open hole in his chest, blood pouring out of it like water. He had the split-second vision of his life, what might've happened if he wasn't about to die. He let out a watery, choking gasp.

Sticks and rocks crunched under Baxter's boots as he approached. He stepped in front of Cole and squatted down, the shotgun resting on his knees. His emotionless eyes searched Cole's.

"I'll let everyone think a bear got you. I'll make it look like you fought bravely. I think you did."

Cole tried to swing the knife out, but he just slumped and collapsed, too shocked to even feel the pain. Darkness was tugging at him, a warm and promising sleep. He fought, but it was like swimming against gravity.

The last thing Cole saw was his uncle Baxter, sighing over him and saying, "I just hope I didn't ruin your skin."

Two weeks later, two county cops came around looking. Baxter invited them inside, to sit on the family couch and have a cup of coffee. A new ottoman sat in front of them. It was small, but it was the same tawny leather as the couch.

There's something about skin
And all the places it has been.

**SCAN THE CODE
FOR A SCARE**

↓

THE DOOR

"I say we open it," said John. "Just pull back the bolt and see what's in there."

Sarah grimaced. They shouldn't have been down in the cellar in the first place. It was off limits. If their dad came back early and found them, they wouldn't be allowed to have screen time for a week. And going through this second door at the back of the cellar—a door they'd never even seen before—well, that was bound to cause even more trouble.

John cast his phone's flashlight at the slatted old door in the gray brick wall. It was nothing more than four long planks of warped wood nailed together.

"It looks ancient," Sarah said. Her mouth was dry, and she didn't like the feeling. "John, do you remember the last time we came down here?"

Her brother nodded. "That's why we're being brave today. To make up for it."

She had felt like a coward that day as they'd fled back up the stairs and into the safety of the house. But they'd only been scared by a shadow. Maybe a mouse or a rat, they'd decided after the event. Once they'd gotten back up the stairs and shut and locked the cellar door, pressing their bodies hard against it, they'd even laughed.

"I don't remember," Sarah began, "there being another door down here. Do you?"

John shrugged. "No, but we weren't down here for very long. We could have missed it."

Sarah didn't think so. They'd been down there at least a few minutes. How could they have missed a whole door in the middle of a wall? The cellar was small and square—there wasn't much to explore other than their dad's tools and a few old boxes containing toys from their childhood.

"So?" John asked. "Are we going to be brave this time?"

Sarah thought they'd already been brave enough by coming down here. But John had that wild look in his eyes, a look of fiery excitement that couldn't be snuffed without his curiosity being sated. "You do it," Sarah said. "You pull back the bolt. I'll wait here."

"Deal."

Sarah watched as John crept toward the door, his footsteps hushed against the huge stone slabs. He moved his hand to the lock, his fingers touching the metal.

The door rattled.

John jumped back, tripping over a box, and scrambled over the floor toward his sister.

"Did . . . did you see that?" he asked, getting back to his feet.

"I think we should get out of here," Sarah said, looking up the stairwell behind her, at the open cellar door.

"Yeah, I think you're—"

A shout from inside the house cut them him off. "Johnathan? Sarah? I'm home. You'd best be in bed!"

"Dad's back," said Sarah, her terror doubled. "Now what do we do?"

John, who always seemed to have an idea, looked thoroughly stumped. Eventually, after a long moment's consideration, he said, "If we go up there, we're dead. Dad will kill us. But maybe he won't check our rooms if he thinks we're sleeping."

Sarah nodded. "Yes! Then we can sneak out of here and get into our beds, and Dad will never know we came down here at all."

Thud.

"That . . . that was the door again." Sarah whimpered, arms trembling.

"No," hissed John, pointing his flashlight up the stairs. "At least, it wasn't the door down here. Look, Dad's closed the cellar door."

"Oh god," said Sarah, as she watched John ascend the stairs. "That's even worse! Please tell me he hasn't locked it."

But John could only shake his head as he turned the old handle. They were trapped.

"We need to knock," Sarah said. "He has to know we're down here, so he can let us out."

"Then we'll have no social life for a month, Sarah. Is that what you want?"

It wasn't. But she didn't want to be down here, either. Not for a moment longer. Why hadn't they listened to their dad? He'd told them to never, ever come down here. He'd even blockaded the door at one point.

"I've got an idea," said John.

"What?"

"That other door—it must lead somewhere. Maybe outside. If so, we can go out through it, then climb back in through my bedroom window."

"I don't think it leads outside," Sarah said.

"Well, let's find out. Right now, it's our best option." John carefully walked back down the stairs.

"What about the bang we heard? What do you think that was?"

"I think the wind rattled it. It's old and loose, and it happened about the time Dad came home. Maybe it was an air current from when he opened the front door."

Sarah considered John's proposition. It seemed like a reasonable explanation. Besides, there couldn't be anything down here, not really.

"Okay," she said. "Open it."

Her brother nodded and approached the wooden door. The beam of his flashlight fell on the wooden slats. There were gaps between them, almost big enough to get a finger through, but his light couldn't puncture the darkness between them.

John pulled back the rusty iron bolt. Then, he paused, as if waiting for the door to fly open and something terrible to come out.

But nothing did.

"See?" said John. "It's just a door."

"Go on, then," Sarah whispered. "See where it goes."

John opened it. The door creaked as he pulled it back. "Wait here," he said. "I'll make sure it's safe." He slipped behind the door and into the darkness.

Sarah waited, shivering. It was pitch-black without John's flashlight, and the cellar seemed to have grown colder since that door had been opened. Perhaps it really did lead outside.

She waited. And then waited a little longer still.

Eventually, she called out, "John? Where are you? What's behind the door?"

"It's okay," came a voice. John's voice, of course, but he

sounded a little croaky. Was he coming down with something? "Just come toward the door. Follow my voice. It leads outside so we're going to be fine."

Thank goodness, Sarah thought as she stepped forward. She entered the pitch-dark space, reaching forward blindly.

Then the door slammed shut, and Sarah heard the bolt slide across the wood.

A flashlight clicked on. It shone on a man's face. Sarah screamed. It was only then that she realized the face was her dad's.

"I told you both never to come down here," he snarled.

He barely looked like the father they knew, the one who played soccer with them on Saturdays and made pancakes in the morning. Now he wore a long red robe with a hood, and his face was shrouded in shadow. Behind him, Sarah could just make out a small table against the wall. It held a worn-looking book, half-used candles, and several large bones. At the edge, Sarah thought she could make out a human skull. The wall itself was painted black, and there were words written in spray paint above. It dripped down the wall like blood.

It read: ALL HAIL BEELZEBUB

"Daddy?" Sarah whimpered.

But her father's scowl deepened. "You defied me. You defiled *this.*" He swept his arm through the room. The light finally touched the far corner, and she saw that John was tied to a wooden stake, his mouth gagged with a sock. Her brother was standing in a stone cavern with a small opening at the top. Was that . . . a hearth? Underneath him, there were logs, twigs, and straw piled high. Her father lit a torch and set it in a bracket on the wall. *Oh no.*

Did that mean . . . ?

Her brother's eyes went wide, and he began to whimper.

"Now you must pay."

"I'm sorry! We'll go!" Sarah screamed, but it was too late. Her father was already tying up her hands.

It was only then that she noticed the tears in his eyes. "It's too late, Sarah. I tried to warn you, but you didn't listen. Beelzebub demands a sacrifice."

There once was a golden door
A tap . . . tap . . . tap, too loud to ignore
Open if you want
But have some faith
This door was shut to keep you safe

SCAN THE CODE
FOR A SCARE

SISTER

I was the only one up late that night. Just me alone on the living room couch, with Netflix and a bowl of popcorn on a Saturday night.

It was well past midnight when a gentle but urgent knocking sounded at the front door. I froze.

My phone buzzed. I reached for it. The tension unwound from my chest. It was a text from my sister: let me in.

I considered making her wait. After all, she'd been nearly an hour late picking me up from gymnastics last week because she'd been "busy." Between you and me, I know my sister wasn't busy doing anything important. I was the one who worked hard, got straight As, committed myself to sports and hobbies, and was going to end up at a good college.

"The golden child," Vera always mocked with a sneer. What can I say? She wasn't wrong. But she also never did anything to help her case. If I had to guess, she'd probably been out doing stuff my parents wouldn't approve of: partying, smoking unknown substances, drag racing, who knows.

I swung open the door to find her hunched under the porch stoop.

I rolled my eyes. "Forgot your key again?"

My sister cocked her head at me. Her eyes looked vacant and strange. I wondered if she was high or drunk. All I could think was how lucky she was that our parents were already asleep.

My frown deepened into a scowl. "Where have you been?"

She didn't answer. Instead, she just stared off into the darkness before turning her head back toward me. Vera had never been stylish, but I'd never seen her dressed like this, in all black. It gave her a strange, almost otherworldly vibe.

"Am I allowed to come in?" she asked.

I paused. Narrowed my eyes at her. She stood stiffly on the porch, soaked through by the rain. Her dark hair hung limp, like a veil half hiding her face. And maybe it was the porch light, but her normally tanned skin looked pale and sallow. Haunting, almost. It was unsettling.

"Mom and Dad are asleep, if that's what you're asking. But Mom said you'll be in trouble in the morning."

I tried to hide my smug grin. It was infuriating how much Vera got away with when I was expected to perform well. Nobody ever talks about the downside of being the golden child. I was tired—physically and emotionally. It was time for Vera to pay for always getting to do what she wanted. I turned and walked back toward the stairs.

Outside, thunder cracked loudly. I turned around as lightning illuminated the still-open door and the long shadow of my sister, standing there.

I paused. She was just . . . waiting in the doorway. Staring at me with bloodshot eyes.

My belly turned. She seemed more than just high. I wondered if she'd been slipped something.

I crossed back to the threshold and reached for her. Her forearm was impossibly cold, even through her jacket. How long had she been outside?

Vera licked her lips.

"Come on," I said, softening. "Get out of the rain."

She crossed over the threshold and peered around the dark living room as if it were a strange museum. The look on her face was wholly alien.

I shut the door behind us. This close, in the low light of the television, I could just make out the dark blossom of a bruise on her throat.

"Were you out partying?" I ventured. That would make Mom and Dad mad.

"Is there anyone else here?" she asked, as if I hadn't said anything.

"What are you talking about?" Uncertainty turned in my belly. "Are you on something?"

Her stare knifed into me.

My breath caught. Suddenly, I understood why her eyes looked so empty and strange. Her pupils were huge and flat, bound by a thin ring of crimson. But she didn't answer. She only stepped closer, enough for me to smell copper on her breath.

"What is wrong with you?" I whispered.

Vera smiled. Her upper lip curled back to reveal a pair of impossibly sharp canines.

A horrible realization sank in my gut: this wasn't my sister anymore.

"No, Sister, the question isn't what's wrong with me," she said, a devilish grin forming on her lips. "I've been *wrong* for years. Nobody loved ugly, stupid, talentless Vera. No . . . everyone only had eyes *for you*."

She took a calculated step toward me, and I instinctively stumbled back, bumping into a side table and knocking over a glass of water. It shattered on the hardwood floor.

"I've spent years not measuring up. Always overlooked. Only good for shuttling my perfect sister to school, to practice, to events. But that's all about to change. I'm finally good for something." She was now a few feet away from me; I searched the room for an escape to no avail.

I backed up farther, my bare feet catching a shard of the splintered glass. Pain shot up my foot and I gasped. I looked down and a small bead of blood smeared on the ground beneath my foot.

My sister's nostrils flared, her head cocked to one side. "Time I finally got the upper hand, Sister."

Only three feet of precious space between us. Nowhere to run. I opened my mouth to scream.

The vampire lunged.

Sister, sister, oh so sweet
Are you more than blood and meat?

**SCAN THE CODE
FOR A SCARE**

FLIGHT 3541

My mother died a year ago. Or maybe not. No one can say for sure. She disappeared off the face of the planet with three hundred other passengers when the Boeing 747 she was flying on simply . . . blipped out of existence.

Somewhere over the Atlantic Ocean, my mother vanished.

But when pieces of the plane started washing up on islands and beaches all around the possible crash site, we knew the worst had happened.

We spent the weeks afterward mourning in our own way. My father disappeared inside himself and spent his days locked in the bedroom they used to share. My sister was out at all hours, avoiding me, avoiding Dad, avoiding the hot cloud of heartache that still hung about our house.

And I kept everything going as smoothly as I could. Someone still had to deal with all the meals and cleaning and bills, even if my father was too heartbroken for it.

My mom used to joke that she was the glue that held our family together. She was right. We'd all relied on her, me most especially. She and I had always been close. My older sister was rebellious and headstrong. She wanted to be her own person. But me? I wanted to be just like my mom.

We had the same mousy brown hair and the same milk chocolate eyes. My grandma used to say I was Mom's "mini-me," and I'd always blushed from the compliment. Mom taught me how to make her famous banana bread, and we watched movies together every Monday night. She held me tight when someone called me "chubby" at school. She was the person I confided in about my first crush.

We were best friends. So when she was suddenly gone, I knew it was up to me to be the family's glue.

Weeks passed, then months. Soon, the one-year anniversary of her death was upon us. As usual, that morning I set out breakfast cereal that my sister barely touched and my dad ate in silence. Both of them left for the day without clearing their bowls, without saying "Bye, Emily" or muttering a word of thanks. By now, I was used to it. Honestly, feeling numb was easier than feeling anything at all. It seemed we'd all agreed on that somewhere along the way.

I checked my phone and saw an email from the airline marking the "tragic" anniversary of Flight 3541, renewing their condolences, and "honoring" the souls on board that "fateful" day.

I deleted the email in disgust.

I decided to skip school. It didn't feel right to spend the day studying trig and watching skit reenactments of *A Midsummer Night's Dream* in English. Instead, I flopped onto the couch and flipped through Netflix for something mindless. I paused on *Gilmore Girls*. It had been our favorite show to watch together. My mom had gotten me into it. She said it was "perfect."

I was alone in the house, three episodes deep, when I heard the knock on the door.

There, on the doorstep, stood my mother, as if she had never disappeared at all. She wore the same outfit she'd had on that morning when she'd pecked a hurried kiss to the top of my head and told me she was going to be late for her flight. Same bag. Even the same shoes.

I just stared at her, mouth ajar.

"Sorry," my mom said. "Forgot my wallet."

For a moment I could only stand there, opening and closing my mouth. Terrified of breaking the spell. Heartache and disbelief rolled in my chest.

Was I dreaming? I blinked several times, trying to wake up, but the daylight streamed in, warming my face, and the tile floor felt cool on my bare feet. I *felt* awake.

Was she real? I wondered impossibly. And if she was, how could she show up after all this time? How did she survive? And why did she look as if not a day had passed since her plane vanished?

Her nose crinkled in that familiar way that made my chest ache with longing. "What's that look for?"

"What the hell happened to you?" I managed.

My mother scowled. "That's a rude question, young lady."

"No, I mean . . ." I trailed off, trying to find some way to explain to her that she might be a ghost. "You were on that plane that disappeared a year ago today." I said this like it was obvious. One long year since my family was irreparably broken.

Now my mother looked at me like I was the mad one. "Honey, I've only been gone twenty minutes. I turned around when I realized I forgot my wallet. Are you okay? Do you have a fever?"

I considered my options. I wanted to believe her. So badly. If she was a dream or a hallucination or a ghost, I didn't want to break the spell.

So I didn't.

I just stepped aside and let her into the house. Her scowl turned into a grin as quickly as it formed. "That's more like it, sweet pea."

A lump formed in my throat at hearing my mom call me by my nickname.

"Uhh, hey, Mom?" I called.

"Yeah?" she yelled back from the office. Wooden desk drawers opening and closing echoed in the hallway. I walked down the hall toward the door, half expecting her to disappear as quickly as she came.

And yet, there she stood behind the desk, her hair askew from bending over, looking for her wallet. Her gaze met mine, and my breath hitched. She looked so effortless, so beautiful. I missed her so much. Enough to make a decision.

"Can we reschedule your flight?" I asked quietly, giving into the fantasy. "I just really need some Mom time."

At this, her expression softened, and she walked toward me with her arms outstretched, enveloping me in a hug. "Oh, sweet pea. What's wrong? Is everything okay?"

I didn't answer. Instead, I just soaked up her embrace and sucked in a deep breath. She smelled like Mom: a mixture of the outdoors and her lilac perfume. It made me want to cry. I let out a shuddering breath. If this was a dream, I never wanted it to end.

Mom pulled back and looked at my face. "You know what? Losing my wallet must be a sign from the universe. I'm calling a mulligan. We'll reschedule my flight for tomorrow and spend the rest of today watching *Gilmore Girls* together."

I beamed.

We snuggled on the couch in our usual way. She sat on one end with her feet propped on the coffee table, and I lay with my feet resting on her lap. We sat in blissful peace for hours. Eventually

I stopped worrying about what this was or how it happened. I just let it be.

But all too soon, my stomach gurgled. I peeled myself off the couch, and Mom turned to me. "Should we make peanut butter and jelly sandies for lunch?" she asked. Her voice was sugary sweet, like a shared secret.

And this was what stopped me in my tracks. I met her gaze, hoping she'd burst out laughing and say, "Kidding, of course." Because my mother was deathly allergic to peanuts. We couldn't even bring food in the house with a warning label that it "may contain peanuts."

But the woman on the couch just smiled up at me expectantly.

"You're not in the mood for PB&J?" she asked. "I always am."

I stared back and suddenly began questioning everything.

"You're allergic to peanuts . . . *Mom*," I said carefully.

Her expression flickered for a moment before regaining composure. "I don't know what you're talking about."

A distant memory of Dad rushing to her side with an EpiPen at one of my soccer games flashed through my mind. She *was* allergic . . . right? It wasn't just some weird dream? My mind raced as I calmly walked over to the kitchen. I opened the drawer on the end and, sure enough, there was an EpiPen sitting right there with my mom's name on the pharmacy label.

The fantasy shattered, along with my heart. And something I knew all along suddenly crystallized in my mind: This woman couldn't be my mother.

Just then, my dad's car pulled into the driveway, and a flutter of panic coursed through me. I needed to get this . . . person out of the house before my father saw her. If he did, I knew he'd believe the lie all too easily. After all, I had. Who knew what this woman really wanted?

"You need to leave," I said with as much authority as I could muster.

"What has gotten into you, sweet pea?" The doppelgänger stood up and started toward the door.

I threw my arm up to block her. "Out the back," I insisted.

The woman just scoffed and tried to push past me. "Emily, you're being ridiculous."

I stepped in front of her again, repeating, "You need to leave. Now. You're no longer welcome here."

My not-mother raised her eyebrows. "Is that how you welcome back your long-lost mother?"

My gaze narrowed. "Are you long-lost? Or have you been gone twenty minutes? Which is it?"

Now my not-mother's irritation slipped. She smiled a slippery, snakelike smile I had never seen before. Dread prickled up the back of my neck. It was like seeing someone else moving in my mother's skin. Uncanny. Horrifying.

"Maybe I had a head injury. Maybe it's a miracle." She nodded down the driveway. "Which one of us do you think he'll believe?"

I looked into her eyes and only now noticed they were darker than mine. An entirely different shade of brown. A stranger stared back at me.

She gripped my arm hard enough to leave red imprints of her fingers and threw me back against the entryway wall.

My dad's key fumbled in the lock.

She smiled and cocked her head. "Now be a good dear and welcome Mommy home."

Down the rabbit hole you go,
Spiraling and spiraling below
Falling from the sky
Is a forever goodbye
Oh, how I wish they'd know.

SCAN THE CODE
FOR A SCARE

↓

THE BONE FAIRY

This one had the most perfect teeth. They had to have cost him a fortune in orthodontics and whitening chemicals. Every time he flashed a smile at me as we walked, those teeth gleamed like pearls.

I didn't usually get this lucky on the first day of school. As the new girl, you'd think some of the boys would resist the temptation to move this fast. After all, I'm just a stranger messaging them on social media between classes.

I wondered if the rest of him was just as pale and perfect, hidden there under his skin.

"You know," I said, popping my Dubble Bubble gum, "my parents would be very interested in those."

"Sorry?"

His smile was lovestruck and bemused as he led me to his "secret spot" beyond the football field. To get there, we had to pass under the bleachers. Initials in hearts carved into the underside of the metal seats reflected off his phone's flashlight. The afternoon sun peeked through the gaps in the benches.

"Your teeth," I clarified.

I smiled, and he mirrored the look, showing me those perfect bones again.

There was a real joy in it, feeding him warning signs for the petty delight of watching them sail over his head, unnoticed. I always liked to watch them stitch it all together at the end. All the little bits of foreshadowing.

"Oh, okay, um . . ."

"They're dentists," I explained.

"Right, yeah. One of those."

My smile stretched thin, thinking about how easy they had it. "This will be easier when I take over their practice."

That one, too, whizzed past him. He simply giggled and gripped my hand harder, leading me past the edge of the dark football field. The school felt empty finally. Peaceful.

"Here it is!"

He announced it so proudly, you'd think we'd be looking over a beautiful beach or cityscape.

"Wow," I responded. Hopefully, my reaction was sufficient. After all, we were standing in the groundskeepers' shed filled with lawn mowers, choppers, and, well, a sinister smell. Even for me.

"What do you think?" he said.

I took his hand. His fingers were hot. I kept rubbing my fingers over his knuckles, testing the bones underneath.

He stared at me with those shallow, empty eyes humans so often have. A blank cow stare.

I squeezed his fingers. "It's perfect."

He kept blabbering on, talking about how unique I was, and how happy he was that I transferred to this school. He was still living in that happy bubble of his.

Funny, I thought.

With each compliment, I recalled several times he'd commented almost the exact same words on countless other girls' social media posts. Did these lines really work on people? I let him float along in his merry stupor as I peered out the windows making sure we were alone.

"You know," he said, his words train-wrecking together, "I

almost didn't respond to your DM. There are so many bots these days, everyone seems fake. Not you, though." He chuckled.

"You sure?"

Behind me, his hands reached for my waist.

"Are we all alone?"

He gave a dopey giggle. "No one ever comes out here."

I pulled him closer by his shirt collar and pressed my mouth to his.

I pushed him into the space between the mowers, until his back hit the old wooden wall behind him. He stumbled and laughed but put both his arms around me to pull me closer.

That was when I let my glamour slip. I had worn the guise of a pretty, young thing—slender, tight clothes, Instagram perfect—but when he pulled away from our kiss, I let him see what I truly was.

His face warped. He had the most delicious confusion, panic, uncertainty. "Something's wrong with you, or something's wrong with me . . ."

I blinked back at him. I knew how I looked. Mottled gray skin, a face like death. He was right to fear me.

He tried to push me away by my shoulders, but I gripped his wrists. Now he could see the talons of my real fingernails.

"What are you?" he cried.

"I'm the bone taker and the bone maker." I sunk my fingers in, under his flesh. It gave like jelly. "They call me the Bone Fairy."

He crumpled, opening his mouth to bleat for help, but I never gave him the chance to speak.

My fingers found the slippery ridge of his radius. I sunk my claws into him and pulled out his bones like I was deboning a fish that was still alive and wriggling. His face collapsed like an empty paper bag. He deflated, all limp skin holding in muscles and organs that tumbled together in the wet sleeve of his body. His eyes were a pair of marbles rolling across the concrete. If his larynx worked, he would still be screaming.

I dipped my hand into the useless sack of his mouth and pulled out a handful of bloody teeth. I used his shirt to clean off my forearm. Tooth fairies always struggled to come by the freshly formed young adult ones.

His bones sat at my feet. I picked one up and gave it a testing flex. They were strong, well-fed. They would sell well. A good day for the Bone Fairy, I decided.

I gathered up his bones in my arms and sauntered off to find my next victim.

SCAN THE CODE
FOR A SCARE
↓

A Riddle

I can be silver, gold, and white
I am born not grown
I am hidden by many and collected by few
What am I?

REDDEST ROSE

The roses were getting thirsty again. So Mrs. Beauregard ran another Help Wanted ad in the newspaper. She only needed new stock every few months.

Mrs. Beauregard designed the ad to target the people most likely to fit the job description. She was not a woman who cared for wasting time.

> **WANTED:**
> **FLOWER SHOP ASSISTANT.**
> *Available to work irregular*
> *hours in irregular ways.*
> *Looking for a long-term position.*
> *No previous experience necessary.*
> **WALK-INS WELCOME.**

Below it, she included a sketch of a single bloodred rose.

These types of ads did not bring her a vast selection, but it did bring her the right sort of people. Considering the odd hours, many were young—schoolkids. The desperate, unknowing kind.

Mrs. Beauregard was mopping the back room of her flower shop when she heard the front bell ring. She dropped the mop in its bucket and wrung out the rusty water. She wiped her hands off on her apron and shuffled to the door.

A girl stood in front of the flower case by the register. Maybe fifteen or sixteen years old. Her eyes were huge, fawnlike. She held the newspaper in her hands and stared at the bouquets in wonder.

Mrs. Beauregard's face split in a hungry grin. "Like 'em?" she asked.

The girl leaned so close to the case of bouquets that her nose nearly touched the glass. "I've never seen such red roses before," she murmured, her breath leaving little clouds of fog on the case.

"My signature. I call them Bloodreds, a crossbreed I have been cultivating for years now." Mrs. Beauregard stepped closer and stood beside her. Even the girl's perfume smelled of rose oil and lavender. Mrs. Beauregard knew she would be perfect. She fanned her fingers together and said, already knowing the answer, "What can I help you with today?"

The girl held up the newspaper. "You said walk-ins were welcome," she said uncertainly.

Mrs. Beauregard nodded and clapped her hands, doing her best to mute her anticipation. If she bit down too soon, she would only scare the fish away. Like a good hunter, she waited.

"They are," she reassured her. "You're here to interview? Splendid. Follow me, please." She inclined her head toward the back room.

"Don't you want to know my name?" she said.

Mrs. Beauregard didn't even hesitate. "Of course," she answered smoothly. She extended her palm. "Forgive me. I am called Mrs. Beauregard."

"Ellie," the girl answered, returning the handshake.

Mrs. Beauregard led Ellie to the back room. She was grateful she had taken the time to clean it up. Her interviewees always became alarmed if they saw the mess from the one before them. At least, the ones who were good at connecting the dots did.

Ellie looked around uncomfortably, her ears reddening, but she wasn't bold enough to turn away. That was a good sign.

Mrs. Beauregard let the door shut behind them. She nudged a tiny metal bar with her foot, locking the door from the inside.

Ellie didn't even notice the slight skip in her step. She just gaped around the room and asked, "Where's your greenhouse?"

"If you're selected," Mrs. Beauregard told her with an impish smile, "I'll let you see it." She inclined her head toward the opaque plastic sheets, partitioning off the flower room. "A woman has to protect her trade secrets. You understand."

Ellie raised her eyebrows. "I wasn't aware florists have trade secrets."

"I'm one of the few," she said with a wink.

Mrs. Beauregard let Ellie look around. There was nowhere else for her to go. She straightened the collar of her blouse and gestured to the table in the center of her workroom, which was littered with discarded stems and trimmed thorns. Ellie sat in the chair facing the door, while Mrs. Beauregard sat in the other.

She always kept herself between them and the door.

"The job is full-time," she told her, "and requires a certain level of physical health to maintain it."

"Physical health?" The first sign of worry crinkled Ellie's eyebrow, deliciously.

Mrs. Beauregard licked her lips. "Are you diabetic or do you have any history of low blood pressure?"

"No," Ellie said, uncertainly.

"No anemia, right?"

"Um. Not that I'm aware of."

"Good, good." Mrs. Beauregard grabbed a clipboard from off the table and pretended to write on it. Ellie could not see her hand move behind it, dipping down into her jacket pocket.

"I just don't see what that has to do with flowers."

"Flowers are surprisingly sensitive to different nutrient sources. I try to keep it as consistent as I can."

Ellie looked like she was trying to make herself smaller. As if that would save her.

Mrs. Beauregard stifled the impulse to chuckle at her. "Do you have any questions for me?" she asked, barely keeping her face straight. She closed her hand around the cold metal in her pocket. It was heavy, but the weight of it made her blood buzz with anticipation.

"Uh. Yes? About everything?"

"Don't worry about it. You're hired."

"What? I don't even know what the job is."

"That's quite all right. I do." Mrs. Beauregard pushed herself away from the table and gestured to the plastic curtain. "Allow me to show you what I need you for."

Ellie stood, clutching her tote bag and looking at the door like she was trying to think of the right way to excuse herself. Mrs. Beauregard watched, her belly twisting with a thrill, as fear of danger and fear of being impolite warred on Ellie's face. So many people walked into that room when their every instinct told them not to, just to avoid offending her.

The irony of that was one of Mrs. Beauregard's darkest pleasures in this job.

"Come along," she insisted.

Ellie walked through the door to the greenhouse.

"I think I should go home," Ellie whispered.

Mrs. Beauregard whispered back, "You're right." A smile formed. "You should have."

Now Ellie's instincts won over. She tried to open the locked door, slamming her hands against it. Mrs. Beauregard admired the dents and scratches that the girl added to the collection. Ellie spun and flew at her, but in a single practiced move, Mrs. Beauregard flicked out the switchblade and pressed it up to Ellie's throat.

"Inside," she told her. "You have a job to do."

Ellie stumbled in, weeping now. The delicate skin of her throat pulsed against the tooth of the knife.

Mrs. Beauregard reached out and lifted the heavy bar, fastening her greenhouse door shut.

The flowers opened up their petals to greet her. Roses grew in thick, perfect clusters in their pots. The petals were an impossible red, blackened scarlet, color of old blood. Even the leaves and stems were dark.

"It's a unique color," Mrs. Beauregard said. She plucked a roll of duct tape from a wicker basket on a shelf beside the door. If the girl had looked into the basket, she would've seen the other tools she kept in easy reach. Rope, pliers, knives, plastic tarps. She pulled out an apron and slipped it over her head, tying it in back and making sure it covered her clothes.

Ellie began to wail and scream.

"Please, darling, you'll upset the plants." Mrs. Beauregard winced. "It's a soundproof room. You'll only make yourself die with a headache."

Ellie's wet eyes scoured the room for an exit. Then she went even paler as she twisted, staring at the far corner. A heavy metal hook hung from the ceiling, a pair of handcuffs suspended from it. Below it sat a metal basin, stained copper.

"I won't tell anyone," Ellie insisted.

Mrs. Beauregard's face split with something like pity. "I'm sorry. They're hungry." She gestured around at her roses. "You understand there's always a higher sacrifice for art."

She advanced on her, knife at her side.

"Please," Ellie sobbed, "please."

Mrs. Beauregard chuckled to herself, knowing the knife was only for show. It's not like she was a murderer.

"Don't worry. They always make it quick."

Mrs. Beauregard handcuffed Ellie to the hook.

If anyone had been in the flower shop, they would have only heard a dull thud. They would not have heard Ellie whimpering as a cascade of vines slithered across the floor like snakes after their prey. They would not hear her muffled scream as the plants engulfed her.

But Mrs. Beauregard heard it all.

She stood with her roses and watched the blood waterfall.

It was the loveliest red she had ever seen.

I'm trapped in the house of beauty
Doomed by my seasonal duty
It may not be a house of glass
But shattered I shall be, alas
To wither and die, shriveling beauty

SCAN THE CODE
FOR A SCARE

THE
DARK WEB

....

Have you heard of a place called the dark web? Well, it's real. And it's dangerous. They wouldn't want me to tell you any of this, but this next section tells some of the horrors people have faced because of it. It really is a dark place.

THE GLITCH KING

Tallie found it a few days ago on her way home from school. Graffiti. A dark green pattern sprayed onto an old, crumbling wall. The paint so fresh it stained her fingers when she touched it.

It had looked alien. Four square eyes staring at her, a maze of lines between them. It took her a moment to realize she was looking at a QR code. She'd fished out her phone and scanned the code. It opened an image on her phone: THE GLITCH KING IS WAITING FOR YOU. Beneath that, the address of a private server for one of her favorite games: *VR-Scape*.

Tallie had been playing *VR-Scape* for months. The game was meant to be infinitely customizable, from its characters to its quests to its server rooms. That was part of the fun. It was also part of the risk.

Sometimes people tried to prank you with a stupid meme or tried to write their own horror story into the game. You didn't know what you were going to get when you clicked into someone's creation.

She'd taken the same route home again two days later, but the graffiti was gone. Either washed away in the rain or scrubbed off by hand. But the server address remained a burning curiosity on her phone.

A few weeks later, Tallie's curiosity got the better of her. She sat in bed, VR headset heavy on her head, and launched the game.

Her avatar stood in the launch portal with her buddy Raiden's avatar—who was miles away at his house playing. Their avatars' inventories were stuffed with every weapon and healing potion they could scrounge up.

Join Unnamed Server?

Server Description: The Crown Must Have a Bearer.

Raiden grinned at her, his avatar's smile cartoonish and huge, full of excitement. "Ready?" he asked.

Tallie nodded. The server description blinked back at her like a warning.

They reached out together, their character arms overlapping, and touched Join.

Then darkness spooled around her. Overhead, the sky was the iron gray of a night storm. The dark cutouts of shivering trees stood out against the sky. For all the servers she had jumped into, she had never seen anything like this.

"Raiden?" she whispered.

Only the trees answered, a low buzzing that seemed to come from everywhere.

She was alone.

Tallie gestured to summon the menu screen, but it wouldn't open. Even long-pressing the power button on the side of her headset did nothing. She wanted to rip off the headset, but her hands froze when she tried.

She kept telling herself, *This isn't real. It can't be real.*

"Raiden!" she called again. "This is a bad joke!"

The trees shifted around her. The scenery chugged forward, slowly at first, then rocketing past her, until the trees were blurs of rushing static, screaming all around.

Not real. It's not real.

At the end of the tunnel of light, a dark shadow appeared.

Recognition spun hot and sick in Tallie's belly. It was the image that had called her here in the first place. The faceless, faintly human shape was darkness cut out of darkness, its head spiked with the knifelike tips of a crown. She somehow knew it was watching her. Waiting.

A mechanical voice hissed through her headset speakers, oily against her ears, "I KNEW YOU WOULD COME, TALLIE GABLE."

Tallie shrieked. She turned and bolted, but it was like running through water. The thick, sludgy air pulled at her as the silhouette drew closer and closer.

"NO MATTER WHERE YOU RUN, THE GLITCH KING WILL FIND YOU."

Someone tugged her headset away. Her bedroom light washed over her, and Tallie startled back to reality like breaking to the surface of deep water.

"What on earth are you doing? It's the middle of the night."

Tallie stared up at her father's bewildered and annoyed face.

Just a game. It's just a game.

"Sorry," she managed.

Her father shook his head and muttered as he walked out of the room, "You're spending too much time playing that game."

Tallie's heart raced, as if some part of her mind was still trapped in that server. It took her hours to fall asleep after she flicked off her bedroom lights.

She did not see the dark shape puddling out from her VR headset. Already taking form, bit by bit. Pixel by pixel.

She could not see the Glitch King oozing to life.

"Where did you go last night?" Raiden demanded at lunch the next day. They didn't have a shared class until fourth period, so it was the first time Tallie had seen him since the night before.

Tallie scowled. Her mind felt half-gutted after that restless night. Her dreams were full of staticky trees with the Glitch King always a step behind her. No matter how quickly she ran, it was there, reaching for her.

"Where did I go?" she said. "Where did *you* go?"

"When we tried to join that server, you logged out. Just vanished." He picked up a piece of cafeteria pizza and said with his mouth full, "And that dumb code didn't even work, by the way. I tried forever after you went AFK."

Tallie opened her mouth to reply, but something just over Raiden's shoulder made her stomach go cold.

A dark shape loomed in the corner of the cafeteria.

That robotic voice echoed through her mind, THE CROWN MUST HAVE A BEARER.

Tallie blinked and the silhouette shuddered impossibly closer. It stood between two lunch tables crowded with chattering high schoolers, but no one even looked at it.

No one saw it. No one but her.

Raiden's brows came together in confusion. "What?" He looked in the direction she was staring. "What is it? Did Mike put beans up his nose again?"

But when he looked back, Tallie was already gone.

She fast-walked down the hall, past tenth graders who side-eyed her, appraising her for ninth-grade weirdness. But Tallie had no room in her mind to wonder if their scoffing giggles were directed at her.

Because when she looked back, the Glitch King followed her like a living shadow.

She started to run now. Faster. Tallie threw herself at the doors leading outside as that voice howled in her head, THE CROWN MUST HAVE A BEARER.

The autumn wind yanked her hair across her face. Tallie smoothed it away and, in the corner of her eye, saw the Glitch King pressed against the glass of the door. She watched the crowned figure pass through the door like it was nothing at all.

She whipped her head around, a plan throwing itself together in her mind. A prairie sprawled alongside her high school, and her neighborhood waited on the other side of it.

If she ran fast enough, she could make it home. Rush upstairs. Throw away that game. Smash her headset. Whatever it took for that dark shape to disappear.

Tallie sprinted, shouldering off her backpack as she ran. She did not dare look back, never slowing. Her tennis shoes tore through the weeds that seemed to tug at her like fingers, trying to trip her up.

No one else was around to see the Glitch King rising behind her. It grew and grew, like someone had cut out a hole in the universe, and it was swelling open to devour her whole.

Tallie dared a single glance backward.

She only saw the Glitch King's black fingers, stretching toward her. Its voice bellowed through her like wind through an open window, NO MATTER WHERE YOU RUN, THE GLITCH KING WILL FIND YOU.

Tallie's toe caught on a bramble of weeds, and she fell, palms skidding. Blood oozed from them as she scrambled to her feet.

But it was too late.

The cold dark fell over her like night, and instantly she plunged back into that nightmare world of darkness and staticky trees. She lifted her hands and saw only the Glitch King's hands. Her face was the Glitch King's: featureless, smooth as a stone.

Tallie screamed and screamed, but no sound came out.

When the police went searching for her later, they saw her footprints trailing through snapped weeds, ending suddenly in the middle of the field. But instead of Tallie, they found a terrified boy where she should have been. A thirteen-year-old from the other side of the country who had gone missing months earlier, holding a VR headset.

The boy just kept mumbling deliriously, "The Glitch King. The Glitch King got her."

No one, not even Raiden, thought to look inside the game.

There, the new Glitch King waits for another player to stumble upon her—for the crown must always have a bearer.

A dark web of your untold story
Holds the truth within its knot
You thought there was limitless glory
Now trapped in my sinister plot.

SCAN THE CODE
FOR A SCARE

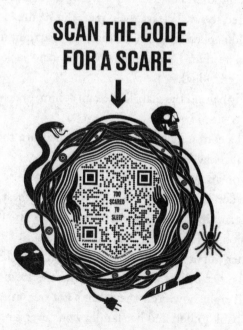

THE CONTROLLER

Felix had never robbed a bank before. And if he ever regained control of his body, he swore he'd never do it again.

"I'm wearing a vest packed fat with explosives," he sneered at the teller—although he didn't want to sneer. Didn't want to say it at all. He wanted to tell her that he'd been possessed by a character from a computer game he played; a character he'd killed in a hundred horrible ways and who was out for revenge. Felix wanted to say, "Please, help me." But he dreaded to think what would happen if he did say that, because right now, he was nothing more than Jack Clancy's puppet. And Jack was a very disturbed individual.

The lady behind the glass looked up at him, eyes wide, pupils dilating. "S-sir . . . ?"

He slid a cotton sack through the gap beneath the glass barrier. "Fill it. Now!"

The woman swallowed hard. "We're quite a . . . a *modern* bank. We don't have much cash. It's all digital these days."

Jack's grinning, half-tattooed face popped up at the top of Felix's vision. A HUD that only he could see.

"Tell her to put her purse in it," growled Jack. "No, not just hers. Make her collect all cash and valuables from the staff. I want it all right now. Tell them, she's got one minute, or you blow the bank to hell and her family won't ever find enough of her body to be able to bury her."

The woman's face had paled. Felix watched her trembling hands as she hugged herself nervously.

"No," whispered Felix. "She's scared to death."

His own right hand flew across his face, stinging his cheek and cutting open his lip.

"Next time you hit yourself, your fist will be closed," said Jack. "Now do as I say."

What choice did he have?

"Gather all your money," Felix demanded. "From you and the rest of the staff. You've got one minute, or I blow this place sky-high."

Jack laughed. His skull tattoo grinning widely. "That's a good lad."

Two hours ago, Felix had been playing *Auto Larceny*, forcing the controllable character—Jack Clancy—to steal a Lamborghini and drive it toward a downtown bridge. Only, the bridge had been rising by the time he'd reached it, so that a ship could sail by beneath.

The car flew off the near-vertical ramp, gliding into the air like a metal eagle. Jack had screamed, but Felix just laughed— he knew the vehicle would never make it across. And indeed it had fallen like an anchor, halfway across the river, plunging into the murky blue depths.

Felix had watched the screen, still laughing, as Jack tried hopelessly, desperately, to shove the car door open. But all that water weighed too much. Instead, the car slowly filled, and Jack gasped, wheezed, and drowned.

Two hours later, waking after a nap, he'd heard Jack's voice in his head. "Hey, Felix. Remember me? I hope you're ready to play another game." Only this time, his body moved without his consent, and Jack Clancy got to call all the shots.

The teller returned, the sack not full, but not empty either. She slid it back to Felix. "It's all we've got."

"Thanks," Felix said, turning and sprinting to the exit.

"You don't thank someone when you rob a bank," said Jack, his face frowning on the HUD.

"Sorry."

"You don't ever say sorry, either. Now, let's find us a car and get the hell out of here before the cops arrive."

Felix burst out the doors and onto the street. Straight in front of him was a parked yellow taxi with the window down.

"Take that taxi," ordered Jack. "And I don't mean rent it. Throw the guy out and drive."

"I'm fourteen," Felix said. "I don't even know how to drive!"

"You've helped me drive plenty of times. Now I'm going to help you."

Felix jogged over to the taxi guy, as if about to ask him how much the fare would cost. Then, in an instant, he reached through the open window and unlocked the door. The driver wasn't wearing a seat belt, and he came out easy, too stunned to react. All he could do was shake a fist from the sidewalk as Felix screeched the taxi into motion.

"Now what?" asked Felix, one hand on the wheel, foot on the accelerator. It felt oddly natural, and he knew why. Because Jack was driving, not Felix.

"We're heading downtown."

The taxi swerved in and out of lanes as it overtook the traffic. Occasionally, it lurched Felix sideways as it nudged other vehicles out of the way.

"Where are we going, Jack?" Felix asked. His palms slipped on the wheel, and his heart tore at his chest each time it beat. "When will you let me go?"

The skull face smiled. "To answer your first question, you know where we're heading. To answer your second question: very soon."

"I know where?"

"You do."

"But I don't . . ." Then it hit him. Hard and cold. He was heading to the river. The bridge. This taxi would become his steel tomb.

"Please don't!" Felix tried to tear his hands away from the wheel, but Jack was fully in control.

"Sorry, Felix. But, listen, at least you only have to go through this once. You know how many times you murdered me in god-awful ways?"

"I—"

"You? You what? I'll tell you: you murdered me a hundred and seventy times, Felix. Drowning was one of the least bad ways to go. So be grateful I'm taking it easy on you."

He could see it now, in the distance. The long slit of blue water. This panic inside of him, the dryness of his mouth, the tears running down his cheeks . . . had he made Jack feel this every time?

"For what it's worth, Jack," he said between sobs. "I'm sorry."

"Sorry?"

"For making you feel all this. Putting you through it. No wonder you're insane. It's my fault."

Jack laughed. "Too late for sorry, kiddo! Hate the game, not the player."

The bridge was half-raised, just like when Felix had been playing the game.

"AHHH!" he screamed as the car soared through the air, slicing the wind. For a second, Felix thought he might actually make it across. Might survive.

Then the car fell.

Plunged into the water.

The ice-cold river poured in through cracks in the doors, slowly filling the sinking car.

It covered Felix's feet, then knees, then chest. He tried to move, to open the door, but he wasn't in control of his body. He was trapped.

Before the water completely covered Felix's face, he glugged out a final "I'm sorry."

Just as everything went black, someone pulled the headset off him. "So? How was it? Do you like your new present?"

Felix trembled. Wiped sweat from his forehead, thinking for a second it was river water. "I . . ."

"Yes?" said Dad, eagerly. His dad.

Felix looked around. He was in his room. At his house. Safe. "The guy at the shop said it was the most realistic *Auto Larceny* game by far. The only one where you're the character and not just controlling a character."

Slowly, it came back to Felix. His birthday. The gift. The game. He let out a deep, relieved sigh.

"So?" said Dad. "Did you like it?"

"Uh, yeah? It was awesome." He snatched the headset from Dad and was about to jam it back over his head when they heard a knock at the door.

"Who could that be at this hour?" asked Dad, walking off.

Felix peered through his bedroom window. He saw a man at the door in his late thirties. He couldn't really make out his face.

Felix's nervous breaths clouded the window. Still anxious from the game.

The man's car, parked in the driveway, looked oddly familiar. Felix felt nauseous. It was the car from the game.

No, it can't be, Felix thought. He wasn't still in the game.

Felix took off running to stop his dad, only to hear a loud thud.

"Oh, Feeeellllliiiiix," the man called diabolically.

"Ready to play again?"

SCAN THE CODE FOR A SCARE
↓

FAME FAKE

Gina sat in bed staring at the doppelgänger on her phone. At her stolen face.

If it was any other morning, she'd have been watching the usual array of popular influencers duetting and dancing on the app's main feed. A feed she had craved to be on, as it led to endless amounts of followers and fame.

But instead of the everyday influencers, she saw herself on the screen. That is, her lips moved and spoke words, but they were words she never would have said. That she *hadn't* said. Because even though it looked like her, sounded like her, it *wasn't her.*

"I know you won't get this, Leo," said fake Gina, "but you're not on my level. You never were. You're trash for what you did to me. It's over! I'm dumping you. And I'll do worse to you . . . soon."

Then Gina—the Gina on the screen—laughed.

But that wasn't her. She wouldn't ever break up with Leo, let alone do it publicly. Even if it meant instant popularity. These days it seemed like every influencer hit their first 100,000 followers with some crazy drama.

Another anonymous text came beeping through. The first message, the one she'd received five minutes ago, had linked her to the video. Told her to visit it through a browser because she wouldn't be able to log into the app anymore.

This second message said:

I made sure Leo saw that video early. I know it seems
sad right now, but I'm going to make you famous. And be
honest, isn't that all you really want?

That last sentence bore through her like a metal spike. *Isn't
that all you really want?*

Because it was true. She'd wanted to be famous for as long
as she could remember. Even before she got a phone, she used
to dress up in front of her mirror and pretend to walk the red
carpet in front of dozens of photographers. She craved a life that
mattered to someone. To anyone. Only now, whoever was doing
this to her was threatening the only person in the world who
mattered to *her*. The only person—besides her parents—who
loved her.

Her heart screamed in her chest as she tried to call Leo. *Pick
up, pick up. Please. You need to know it wasn't me. I'd never say that
stuff!*

But Leo didn't answer. Why would he after she'd publicly
humiliated him? Thousands of people had already seen it. She'd
been posting content for years, mainly dance and reaction videos. She'd accumulated almost 4,000 followers, and in just the
past couple hours, she'd grown ten times that. The video was
spreading so fast, a few real-life friends had even commented on
her fake post, some defending her, others Leo.

You're a liar, Gina, Leo would never have done anything
bad to you.
Gina, what did he do to you?
Omg. Leo, you suck!
Poor Gina.

She needed to calm down. There were other ways for her to
reach Leo.

Except, there weren't.

WhatsApp and Facebook and Twitter and Instagram—she couldn't log into any of them. Gina tried to reset the passwords, one by one, but each time she was informed that her email address had recently been changed.

Gina hadn't changed it, though. Hadn't changed anything. What was happening to her? She thought of a sandcastle on the beach, how perfect it looked until the tide suddenly swept in and collapsed it into a pile of sloppy, wet sludge. She sat helpless as her life turned to sludge around her. Is this what fame felt like?

She kept refreshing her page, watching the follower count grow by the second, now surpassing 150,000. Fifty thousand new followers in just the last three minutes. Was it bad that it made her feel just a *little* bit better? Guilt twisted in her stomach.

Her fingers tapped out a reply to the latest text:

Who are you? Why are you doing this?

It didn't take long for a response to arrive.

Think of me as a genie, granting people like you the wish
they most desire. I've been watching you for a long time
now, Gina. Listening. Learning all about you. What sites you
visit, what trends you follow. I'm more you than you are.

Watching her? Gina trembled as her eyes moved to the camera at the top of her phone. She covered it with a finger, as if that would stop it from having already stolen her image. The video online was a deepfake—her image, her voice, yet it was in no way her.

This person had turned her into a digital puppet.

Another message came through:

You always wanted to be famous, didn't you Gina? I've
seen you crawl Google for ways to get videos to go
viral, to get more views, to get on TV. And I hate seeing

teenagers fail, so I'm going to help you. I'm going to make you famous. But everything has a price.

Another text message. This one from her bank account. The one her parents helped her set up to deposit birthday checks and the small income she got from making videos.

Withdrawal successful.

Oh god, they were taking everything from her: Leo, her friends, her money. She knew, even before she tried her bank's app, that she wouldn't get in. That the details had been changed.

Gina wanted to scream, but what good would it do? Just then, she got a new post notification. She loaded up her browser and checked her stolen TikTok account, praying it was just an error.

But a second video had been uploaded, only minutes ago.

On the screen, fake Gina was grinning. "Just a quick update for you all. Yesterday, I did something pretty risky, but—with any luck—it is going to make me *very* famous. I don't want to give away any spoilers, but just know you're all going to be seeing a lot more of me soon."

Gina watched the video again and again, looped, like a snake devouring its tail. What did the video mean? What had she "done" yesterday?

Her follower count continued to climb, now passing half a million. People were even watching and commenting on her old videos, sending heart emoji and asking for more. All Gina had ever wanted, happening in front of her eyes.

She needed to talk to someone.

To Leo.

Gina could get to his place in twenty minutes. Explain it all. Show him the texts on her phone. Yes, he'd understand, and then he'd help her! They'd go to the police together, report it.

She'd forward him the texts now—before she even left the

house. Give him time to react before she turned up.

Except, when she went into her messages, the texts were gone. They'd been deleted. Permanently.

This person controlled her phone. Controlled everything.

Gina forced herself out of bed—she had to get to Leo. Explain in person. She made it to the bathroom and splashed water on her face, hoping that it might wake her from this nightmare.

A new message:

Where are you going, Gina? Don't leave yet—they'll be here soon. Gina, do you remember saying to Leo: "I'd do anything to be famous." Because I remember. And Leo, didn't he say that he'd do anything to help?

A shiver sailed down her back. What did it mean "they'll be here soon"?

Gina grabbed her bike helmet and headed for the door.

Yes, she'd told Leo she'd do anything to be famous. But it had been a joke. At least, sort of. And Leo had always been supportive. He'd wanted her dreams to come true as much as she did. Gina refreshed her page once more. Her heart fluttered. One million followers. She couldn't help but smile.

She heard the wailing of sirens as she opened the door. A moment later, two police cruisers pulled up.

Thank god. They must have found the person doing this, the person trying to steal her life. They'd come to let her know that everything was okay.

Two men stepped out of the first cruiser.

"Gina Elray?"

"Yes. That's me."

"You're under arrest for the murder of Leo Althwit. Anything you say—"

His voice drifted away as dizziness came over her. Her legs

felt weak and wobbly. The . . . murder?

"I didn't kill Leo," she'd said, numbly, weakly.

The other officer grunted. "Your fingerprints were all over the place. Even on the knife. And you confessed online. That wasn't a smart move, was it?"

She wanted to laugh. They had it all so wrong! It couldn't be Leo dead, and it couldn't have been her fingerprints there because she hadn't been—

Her phone.

Each time she unlocked it, she needed to press a finger against it.

It must save her fingerprints to the phone, she realized. To compare hers to other people's, so that it would only unlock for her.

And if her fingerprints were stored on the phone . . . could someone print them off? Stick them on surfaces? Windows and doors?

A knife?

"He can't be dead," Gina said.

A flash of yellow light dazed her. A camera.

"Reporters are already here," said the first cop. "You're about to become very famous. Hope you're ready for it."

Within moments, photographers swarmed the cop car trying to get a picture of her. Gina thought back on all the times she'd imagined this moment, her debut. She'd imagined it so differently. Nevertheless, she was ready for it. She'd been practicing all her life. It was what she'd wanted more than anything. And now she had it.

She figured she should smile.

There once was a girl who wanted more
Every day felt like a chore
She wished and waited for the chance
When she'd be famous and known at a glance
But fame is a game that can turn to pain
There once was a girl who wanted more

SCAN THE CODE
FOR A SCARE

CONSUMED

I've always hated smartphones. Screens of any kind, really. Something about the blue light makes me squirrelly and anxious. Staring at a screen—especially the kind you can carry anywhere—changes people. You end up pulling them out and skimming social media feeds without even realizing it.

My sister, Margo, used to be like me. We could spend hours drawing or writing or getting lost in make-believe. But today she turned sixteen, and our parents got her a smartphone in a shiny white box.

She squealed with joy, jumping up and down and hugging them and shrieking, "Oh my god, thank you!"

But I just sat there, glaring at the box.

My father elbowed me and teased, "Don't worry, Callie. When you're sixteen, you'll get your first real phone, too."

"I don't want one," I muttered. I had an old-school flip phone that only made calls, and it was all I needed. Even if the other kids at school mocked me for not having a tiny computer in my pocket.

"Jealous much?" my sister said as she ripped the plastic seal off the box.

I scowled and said nothing. But later that night, my sister hadn't touched her other gifts: the new pencils or notebook or the books I had saved up to buy her. She spent all night scrolling away on her phone, her eyes alive with light.

"Good night," I said from my bed in our shared room.

Margot didn't even tilt her head toward me. She just kept scrolling and scrolling. A clown with teeth like glass shards smiled from PicShare post after PicShare post.

I leaned closer and repeated, "Good *night*."

That close to the screen, I could just make out the words: *ANYTHING IS HACKABLE. EVEN YOUR MIND.* Margot scrolled away before I could tell if I had misread it.

"Night," she muttered without looking up.

The change started in her eyes.

My sister had gray eyes, the color of a winter sky. I used to be so jealous of them because my own flat brown eyes felt boring in comparison. If anything, mine were more like dirt.

I noticed it one morning over breakfast a couple of weeks after she got her phone. Her irises were no longer gray; instead, they had a strange bluish gleam. Even when she glanced up at me and away from her screen for half a second, the strange light in her eyes stayed.

"What's the matter with you?" I asked.

"Callie," my father cautioned without looking up from his own phone, "be nice to your sister."

I glared at the toast going cold on the table. My father and sister sat together, but they were so very separate. Neither one of them was speaking, both lost in their screens.

The whole room suddenly smelled like something was burning.

I looked over at my mom, who stood by the stovetop, her thumb mindlessly roving over her phone screen. She didn't even glance at the bacon blackening and smoking in the pan.

"Mom, look!" I said.

"Whatever your father said, dear."

"No, Mom! The bacon! Didn't you notice?"

She blinked like someone coming out of a dream, looked at the pan, and said, feebly, "Oh." Then her eyes were glued back to her phone.

I jumped up and flicked off the stove, moved the pan off the heat. My mother didn't even flinch.

"What is going on with everyone today?" I snapped.

But then I saw it. My parents both had that impossible glow in their eyes, the same as my sister.

"It's you, too," I told them. "Your eyes . . ."

"Hm?" My father wouldn't look up at me now. "Okay, honey, do whatever you need to do."

I followed his stare to his phone, but it wasn't even on anymore. The screen was black, yet his thumb still ran across it, over and over.

Everything reeked of smoke and fear, so I grabbed a couple slices of toast and took off on my bike. It was crazy early for school, but I needed room to think. The autumn wind was cold, but it was as real as the sky that was once the same color as my sister's eyes.

That was comforting. At least some things were still real.

The streets that were usually full of cars and semitrucks were eerily empty, the stoplights standing like fleshless bones. I pedaled through the intersections, feeling like an intruder. Here and there, cars were stopped in the middle of the road. Lights on, engines running.

Their drivers sat with the same glowing eyes, their phones locked in their hands.

I surged past them to school because I didn't know where else to go. My mind spun back to my family.

They had to be better by tonight. They had to be.

The staff parking lot was empty. It was a little past seven a.m., so there should have been teachers here getting ready for the day. Janitors. The office staff flicking on lights and unlocking doors.

But the school was completely unlit. The black windows stared back at me like empty eyes.

When I tried the front door, it was unlocked.

"What is going on?" I whispered.

I'd probably get fifty detentions if any teachers caught me, but something in my gut told me not to leave my bike behind. I wheeled it into the hallway, walking warily beside it. I flicked on the flashlight I'd tied to the handlebars, and it cut a scope of light out of the darkness.

"Hello?" I called. "Is anybody here?"

I crept down the halls. The classroom doors were shut. I searched hallway after hallway and found every room empty. Even the cafeteria, which should have been serving breakfast, was still locked up tight.

I eventually found the janitor, a friendly old man who always ruffled my hair and called me kiddo. He stood in the staff room, holding the vacuum in one hand. But his other hand held his phone, and he stared and stared at it.

"Are you okay?" I ventured.

I tiptoed closer to touch his arm, but he didn't even glance at me. Didn't look up from his phone.

The television in the corner—an old LCD relic from the pre-wall-screen days, when televisions were still measured in inches instead of feet—was flicked on. The *Channel 6 News* ticker ran along the bottom of it, but there were no news anchors. Nothing but words that made my blood run cold:

PUBLIC SAFETY ANNOUNCEMENT: DO NOT LOOK AT YOUR PHONES, WHATEVER YOU DO.

STAY WHERE YOU ARE. HELP IS COMING.

I knocked the janitor's phone out of his hands, as if that would break the spell. It clattered and fell screen-up. I reached up to cover my eyes, but not before catching a half-second glimpse of the screen. There was a glitchy, grinning face on it, a clown that was all sharp teeth. *YOU ARE WHAT YOU CONSUME* repeated over and over in the background

That was all it took.

The pull was magnetic, all-consuming. Like the suck of a riptide, dragging me under. But even as part of my mind screamed at me to close my eyes, my body moved of its own accord. Stooped down. Picked up the phone, its plastic case hot in my hand.

Out of the corner of my eye, I could see myself reflected back in the window. A silhouette with glowing eyes.

I didn't know if anyone would come. And for once, I didn't care.

I loved this rectangle of light more than anything in the world.

SCAN THE CODE
FOR A SCARE

↓

THE GEOCACHE

The asylum stood alone on a road once known as Woods Way, a name long forgotten by both time and society. Its brick exterior lurched lopsided toward its west side, where the marshy ground had slowly swallowed its foundations.

"Pull over by the gate," said Bret, tracking the green dot on his phone's geocache app. "This is it."

Avery parked on the side of the road, but she figured she could have stopped right in the middle and no one would have batted an eyelash—because no one lived out here to bat an eyelash. No cars traveled this road. In fact, they hadn't seen another person in almost an hour.

She looked out the window at the asylum's long, dark silhouette looming beneath a gray sky. A shiver sailed down her spine. "So it really *is* here."

"Looks like it," replied Bret.

They'd checked Google the day before to do a little research on the area, to see what waited for them at the coordinates—but Google came up blank, except for one reference to an old asylum that had once housed mentally unwell people. No Google Street View of it. No other information. That hadn't stopped them. In fact, it made the idea of coming here all the more enticing. If anything interesting waited to be found, they might be the first people to record it.

The name of the cache, of the treasure they were chasing,

was "The Secret of Woods Way." That curious name, plus the coordinates, had gotten them this far. It only had to get them a little farther.

"Come on," said Bret, getting out of the vehicle. "And start recording, will you?"

Avery followed. She held out her phone and loaded up a live stream. "Hey, everyone! Guess where me and Bret are. Yep, we're outside a creepy-as-fudge asylum." She aimed her camera at the building, panning slowly over it, before turning it back on herself. "Freaky, huh?"

Bret butted into the picture, his shoulder pushing against Avery's. "And she doesn't mean her face!"

"Jerk," said Avery, laughing. "But for real, this place isn't even on Google. It's crazy! It's like it's been totally forgotten. Except by the person who added it to the app." She said this last part to Bret, not to their audience, which already numbered in the hundreds.

Bret gave her a questioning smile. "Guess that's true." He looked back at the camera. "We're going to be entering the asylum now because that's where our treasure lies. So come with us, if you dare!" He let out a cackle of pretend-evil laughter.

Avery let Bret walk ahead to the rusted iron gate so that she could film him. Mist rolled by in plumes. She felt like she was shooting a horror film. The gate squealed as Bret pushed it open.

Avery stayed a few steps behind Bret, following him up the dirt path, beneath overgrown willows that hunched and brushed the ground.

A huge silver knocker hung on the door.

"Look at that," said Bret to the camera. Or to Avery. She

wasn't sure. "Think I should knock it?"

Avery shook her head. She didn't think he should even touch it. This place made her uneasy; she thought of a mouse being slowly cornered.

Bret looked at his own phone, scanning the chat room responses. "They want us to knock. Well, I guess it's only polite!" He pulled back the knocker, then sent it flying against the oak timbers of the door.

The thud made them both jump. Bret laughed uneasily. Avery didn't.

"Looks like no one's home," Avery said.

Bret nodded and twisted the handle. "Then we don't need an invite."

The door opened; the stench of mold and mildew, of something rotten and sour, flooded out.

"Ew," said Bret, holding his nose comically. "You should all be grateful that you're not here with—" He stopped. Stood silent.

"What is it?" asked Avery breathlessly.

Bret stared at his phone. "That's really strange."

"What is?" Her heart pumped hard now, as if it sensed something was wrong and was trying to get her legs moving.

"Everyone's left the chat room," he answered. "Like they've been kicked out. Except for one person. Wray01." Bret turned to Avery's phone and waved. "Looks like it's just you and us for now, Wray, until everyone else returns." He watched as Wray01 typed up a reply.

Wray01: Lucky me! Guess my proxy paid off and kept me from getting kicked out.

"Maybe we should wait here, outside, for them all to come

back," said Avery. "I don't want them missing anything." She liked all those eyes watching—not for the attention, but for the comfort. It was like having a hundred security cameras. Nothing bad could happen with that many people watching. "Or better yet, we could come back another day when it's fixed."

"Nah," said Bret. "We'll upload the video after we've looked around. They'll all get to see it. Besides, it took four hours to drive here. I'm not doing it again without a really good reason."

He stepped through the door and into the darkness. Avery followed slowly behind.

In the asylum's vaulted hallway, the sharp scent of urine joined the other unpleasant smells. Avery guessed vagrants had found this place at some point or another. She hoped they weren't still here. Her phone's flashlight darted around nervously, painting shadows on the huge walls.

"This is it," said Bret. "Pretty much the right spot, according to the app. Except nothing—"

Bret pointed at a dark lump on the ground, near the winding wooden stairwell. "Look. Someone's here," he whispered.

So squatters still slept here, she thought. "Bret, we should go."

But Bret was already heading toward the shape; she kept her camera locked on him. "Don't wake him," she hissed. "Please."

"Holy . . ." Bret turned to the camera. "I think . . . I mean, yeah, he's got to be dead."

Avery saw the man. Naked. A long, jagged cut zigzagged from his chest to stomach, peeling it open. A patch of dried blood stained the wood beneath him.

Bret's phone beeped. A member of the chat room must have private messaged him.

Wray01: Well done finding my treasure.

Bret looked at the message, then held his phone up to Avery.

"He . . . he did this?" Avery asked, voice trembling.

Wray01: I always put the bodies somewhere creative.
Somewhere not very visited, that I think is worth a visit.
Then I add them to the app.

Bret stared at the camera, his face pale. "What have you done? Who are you?"

The front door slammed. A click as the lock turned.

"Bret!" screamed Avery.

Bret looked at his phone one last time.

Wray01: Don't worry. I'll find somewhere good for your bodies, too. They'll be found. Eventually.

A map followed
A man unseen
A path swallowed
A faint scream

**SCAN THE CODE
FOR A SCARE**

THE UNEARTHLY, THE GHOULISH, AND THE DOWNRIGHT MONSTROUS

....

These next stories speak for themselves. By now you must know the world is so much more terrifying, so much more wicked than you could've possibly imagined. If you still don't believe me, read on.

THE EXPRESSWAY TO HELL

Thankfully, the train was late.

He looked around to jump the turnstile, then halted. This was the first time they had posted a guard at the entrance. Michael had wondered if it was because of him; he'd been jumping it a lot lately. He looked back and forth to see if the guard was watching him, but no, he was facing the opposite direction. That was Michael's moment. He jumped.

There was an old lady, a bit disheveled, standing nearby. Her nearly black eyes caught his—she'd seen him jump but said nothing.

It wasn't that he needed to sneak on the train without paying, but he had better things to spend his money on than a ticket. Besides, it was exhilarating. He was tired of always doing what he was told. He liked to live on the edge. That's why he was skipping school. School was for losers.

Michael bent forward from the edge of the platform, leaning over the tracks as far as he dared. He panicked as he felt himself lose his balance. For a moment he thought he might fall on the tracks. Then a thin, bony hand grabbed his shirt and pulled him upright.

It was the old woman. When she spoke, her voice sounded as worn as a pair of weathered boots. "You look troubled, boy."

Michael didn't respond, embarrassment burning red in his cheeks. Was she going to confront him about not paying?

Regardless, he planned on tuning her out. Like most New Yorkers, he usually made a habit of acting as if he couldn't see or hear the other people he passed in the streets.

"No one comes down here unless they are," the old woman continued. She wore a long, swooping skirt, tattered and dirty, but the dark purple fabric beneath it bore an ornate pattern like twirling vines. She had a patched-up shawl with knotted tassels. Copper coins going teal with rust clinked from the tassels. She looked like she stole a costume from some theater's storage.

Her face was wrinkled, turtlelike, but her eyes were sharp and earnest. There was no hint of madness in those eyes.

Still, Michael was not about to listen to some strange lady ramble. So instead he just muttered, feeling awkward and faintly guilty, "Sorry, I don't have any change."

"I didn't ask for any."

Light appeared at the tunnel, saving him from this conversation. "This is my train," he told her.

The woman shook her head. Her dark eyes widened into disks. "This is no one's line, boy."

Michael just scoffed and pulled his phone out. No signal. He watched the approaching subway lights and prayed it would come faster.

"That track carries you across the Styx," the old woman hissed. "And there is no uncrossing it."

"The sticks? Lady, do you even know where you are?"

"Do you?" she countered. She stretched her arm out as if inviting him to look around. The coins on her shawl jingled.

Michael twisted his head. For the first time, he realized that, outside of the guard, they were the only two people in the station. During morning rush hour. Creepy. He swallowed hard.

The subway screeched to a stop in front of him. The doors wheeled open. The inside was completely empty, but it looked normal. Brightly lit, the usual amount of mild filth and graffiti. And it had to be better than staying here with this old woman who was really starting to freak him out.

Michael approached the car.

"This is your last chance," she said, putting her thin fingers around his arm. He pulled away hard at her cold touch.

Michael paused in the open doors of the subway. He scowled at her and said, "Take a hint and buzz off next time, lady."

Then he stormed on and plopped down by one of the windows. He could feel the old woman's eyes on him even as the doors closed and the subway pulled away from the station.

It was weird that the train car was also empty at rush hour, but Michael was still preoccupied with the strange encounter with the woman.

The train picked up speed, shuddering as it went faster and faster. Michael was used to the dull roar of the engine rattling along, but this time it just kept accelerating. The walls shook so hard, the very windows trembled. He pulled an energy drink out of his backpack and took a sip. The train rattled again, and he spilled all over his shirt. The bottle slipped from his hand onto the floor, spilling the bright red liquid everywhere. But that was the least of Michael's worries.

The subway rocketed through the darkness, screaming down the tunnel. It veered around the next corner so sharply that Michael was flung from his seat.

What the heck?

And then the lights cut out. The black was so complete, Michael couldn't even see his hands in front of his face. He crawled through the puddle of spilled drink and felt . . . nothing. His pants should have been sticky and wet. But they weren't.

Chills slithered down his neck. He tried grasping for anything in the pitch-black emptiness. Michael felt like a screw was being tightened into his chest with each breath he took.

Then, he heard a chuckle nearby.

Michael scrambled back, letting out an involuntary yelp. Now there was more laughter, spreading in waves throughout the empty car. Like listening to a laugh track play from the conductor's speakers.

The lights flared on. This time they burned a low amber, as if lit by a sulfur fire.

Dozens of faces surrounded him. All of them were human, all transparent. Were these the faces of the dead? Some of them wore clothes that were decades out of fashion. Suits and dresses that looked as old as the subway itself.

"Surprise!" one of the ghosts jeered, and the rest joined in cackling.

Michael scrambled to his feet again. The ghosts shoved and jostled him, laughing, delighting in the way he cried out at them, "Let me out! Let me out!" They did not relent.

"Where are we going?" he asked, terrified.

"Down!" replied a big man in a bloodstained Christmas sweater.

The tunnel began to lighten the farther they went. But the light was a deep, angry red, like the inside of a volcano. It pulsed and churned across the walls of the train like it was testing them somehow. Michael couldn't tell how long they'd been going. Time didn't really seem to matter anymore. But he was certain it had been a while.

When he looked down at his hands, they, too, had become transparent and withered. Oh god, how long had this journey taken?

Finally, the subway stopped. The doors winced open. But no platform was beyond them. Just a raging lake of fire.

Then the raucous laughter and jeering went deadly silent. Every ghost on board seemed to hold their breath.

Michael turned his head to the dead woman beside him. He whispered, "What's going on?"

"It's choosing," she whispered back. Her eyes were haunted, sunk deep into her skull. She wore a stained dress that looked at least half a century old. She tried to make herself as small as possible.

Instinctively, Michael followed suit.

A hand rose up from the flames, with skin like hardened magma. It reached into the subway, its claws screeching and scratching along the windows. Michael felt like a toy about to be crushed by a giant. His grip on the subway pole tightened as though it might save him.

The hand settled on a ghost just a few feet from Michael. It was the man in the Christmas sweater. The man opened his mouth to scream, but the demonic hand hooked a claw through his throat. The only sound that came out was a gurgling whimper.

As quickly as it had appeared, the hand snaked back out, dragging the ghost man down into the lake of fire. And then he was gone.

The doors squeaked shut again. The train heaved away from the station, away from the burning gates, climbing back up into the darkness.

After a time—perhaps a day, perhaps a century—the subway finally looped around. It sighed back into that lonely station. The old woman stood there, just as hunched and brittle as before, beside a man in a business suit who may as well have been Michael what seemed like a whole lifetime ago. The man pretended to look very interested in his watch as the old woman shook her head.

Michael watched it all play out like a pantomime. He pressed his hands to the glass and heard himself whispering to the man on the platform, over and over again, "Don't do it. Don't do it."

But the man stepped on. He didn't see the ghosts crowding the seats, staring back at him with a mix of dread and pity and derision. The ghosts scattered like frightened fish as he selected where to sit. They hovered, watching, murmuring among themselves.

The subway lurched away from the station. Michael turned toward the platform to find the old witch watching him through the glass. Her expression looked like an apology. Maybe she was just as trapped as him. He was doomed to ride, and she was doomed to watch mortal after mortal disobey her earnest warning.

Michael wanted to call this new passenger a fool for not heeding her warning. But he knew deep down that he'd been the fool all along. Too reckless, too blind to others to hear an earnest plea.

The subway thundered on, down into the dark eternity.

SCAN THE CODE
FOR A SCARE

↓

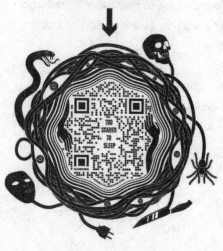

A Toehold

When the time comes
You will know where to go
For what shall be, becomes
Your destiny, to rise above or fall below
Now take the first step, so you know
Cl
imb
ing, up
And up, you go
Until a light touch on the t
o
e

FINDERS KEEPERS

It's not easy being a good thief. You've gotta be confident, clever, quick on your feet. You've gotta believe you deserve it.

I'm only fourteen, but I know the game of life is rigged. Kids like me will always be the school losers. We'll never have the newest sneakers or phones. I don't even ask my parents, because I hear them arguing all the time about rent and bills and my mom's knee surgeries.

Let me show you how to level the playing field. It's a little game I call "Finders Keepers."

I only steal from rich people. Supply and demand, baby. Their supply meets my demand. I show them how it feels to want something they can't have.

Today I'm in the Highlands, which is the richest of the rich neighborhoods. Fancy houses with fancy cars, fleets of landscaping teams humming back and forth, weeding and watering every lawn.

The only landscaping going on in my apartment building are the rats munching away in the walls.

I'm cruising along on my trusty skateboard. It was my first major lift, almost a year ago. Back in those days, I would grab a package off a porch and sprint like an idiot. The skateboard was worth it, but I've evolved my approach since then.

Now I cruise confidently through the neighborhood like I belong. I wear a pair of designer sneakers I lifted a few blocks over and a preppy polo I snatched last summer. My pièce de résistance is a Red Sox baseball cap I found in the school lost and found. None of it is my style, but I look convincing enough to be some rich family's kid. Plus, the hat is good at keeping my face out of view.

It's a bad day for package hunting, honestly. It's already after school, so parents and nannies are home. Backyards are busy, and there are eyes everywhere. I'm close to giving up when I hear a whisper to my left, distinct but soft.

"Hey, kid. Over here."

I snap my head around and see no one.

But there, on the porch to my left, is a black box. I freeze on the sidewalk for a second, scanning, calculating. The house has a For Sale sign, and the front porch is shaded in willow trees.

I jog up the steps, tugging my baseball cap down to hide my face even though the sign gives me an innocent reason to dare a glance inside. Empty. No furniture, nothing. Every surface inside looks eerily white.

I don't hesitate. I hunker down and inspect the box. Its sides are smooth plastic, so black they're practically eating all the light that touches them. It feels heavy, electronic, fancy.

C'mon, it seems to say. *You deserve this.*

I stuff the box into my backpack and scurry down the stairs, absolutely buzzing with delight.

I only score one more box the whole afternoon. It looks like a Styrofoam container that keeps expensive gourmet food cold until rich people decide to look on their porches. It barely fits in my backpack, but I'm hungry, so I grab it on pure impulse. Because I can. Because they don't deserve it, and I do. They don't even appreciate what they have.

It's dark by the time I get home, almost seven p.m. My parents both work late on Wednesdays, so I march straight to my bedroom and lock the door. I'm so jittery with excitement, I just dump out my backpack on my bed. My loot tumbles out. I set the Styrofoam container aside and seize the little black box. I turn it over and over. I can't find a hinge, a lid. Nothing.

The box just sits in my hands, its plastic sides smooth and almost cool to the touch.

I fumble with it for a few more minutes before tossing it aside with a scowl. Before I mess with it further, I cut open the Styrofoam container, to see if it's even worth keeping. But my heart gets all weird and fast because it's not food like I thought. It's medicine in a temperature-safe box. Insulin for someone named Charlotte Wright.

Listen. This is the really hard part.

Sometimes you'll want to take the stuff back when it's something like a toy for a kid or diapers or a book about grief. But remember, rich people can buy anything. Rich people can do anything. It's not my fault they didn't take their package inside if it was important. I can't risk going back and getting caught.

It's not my fault.

"Finders keepers," I remind myself.

I toss the insulin and the packaging into a garbage bag, tie it off, and run it to the dumpster downstairs. The elevators are broken again, so it takes me almost ten minutes to go up and down all twelve flights. I'm panting and hungry when I get back inside. The guilt has worn off, and now I'm just annoyed I had to run around so much.

Those feelings vanish instantly when I walk into my room. I don't remember turning the lights off, but everything's dark.

My breath hitches in shock.

The black box sits on my bed, but now it's open. I look around the room for an explanation. Did my parents come home early?

I stand very still and listen. Our walls are pretty thin. You can hear everything from footsteps to toilets flushing. After thirty seconds of absolute silence, I'm sure they're still at work. My pulse quickens.

I rush forward and peer inside and see . . . nothing.

The inside of the box is as black as the exterior. I shine my phone's light in there, but there are no edges. It looks like . . . a void.

I reach inside, confused, but my hand doesn't touch the bottom. It doesn't touch anything. There's just cold air, the insane feeling that my hand is numb, not even a part of me.

An image rises to my mind, unbidden. An old woman checking her porch, day after day. She looks dizzy and tired. I don't know how, but I instantly recognize her. Charlotte Wright: the woman whose insulin I stole.

I see her standing in a kitchen window framed by gingham curtains. She sways, delirious. I see her fall backward, landing horribly on her arm. Then there's the flurry of ambulance lights, the surgery room, all that blood. Charlotte in a hospital bed, her torso bandaged, her right arm just a stump.

Panic tightens my throat. I'm too scared to scream.

"What's going on?" I say to no one.

Just like that, the image fades. I'm back in my room, but the box is too heavy to move. I'm elbow-deep into it, deeper than the box should go. My arm just disappears into black shadow. No matter how hard I yank, I can't move or feel anything, which is worse than pain.

"I'm sorry." I feel like a loser, but I can't stop crying. "Please, whatever you are. Just let me go."

Now I'm certain I hear a voice. It's laughing as that box sucks my arm in, deeper and deeper. I thrash and scream, but my arm disappears up to the shoulder. Cold tingles up my nerve endings, severing them one by one.

I scream and scream, but there's no one to hear me.

After minutes—or hours—the door flies open behind me. My dad is rushing over, grabbing me, and it's only then that I look down and see it.

My right arm is gone. The stump protrudes from my shoulder, oozing blood, as if it was removed with surgical precision.

"The box," I gasp out, "the box . . ."

"What box, son? What box?"

I point, but my bed is empty. There's just half a Styrofoam lid and my bloodstained sheets and that voice. That voice that directed me and laughed at me is mocking me, echoing through my mind.

"Finders keepers," it croons.

SCAN THE CODE
FOR A SCARE
↓

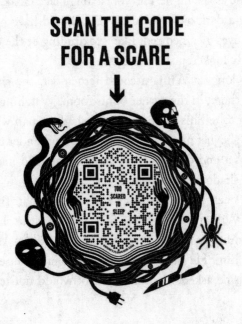

THE SHADOW MAN

There was a shadow man in William's room, but no one else could see it.

William knew the shadow man was invisible because his mother bustled into his room now and then throughout the day to put away laundry or chide William for leaving toys on the floor. But even when the shadow man stood inches from her, William's mom did not so much as flinch. Sometimes she even walked right through him.

The shadow man looked as if he had been cut out of the same fabric as the night. He wore a long black cloak. He had no face, only a dark oval where his face should have been. In the dark, his eyes gleamed red, like a fox hiding at the edge of the garden. He looked just as hungry.

For as long as William could remember, the shadow man had been there, in the corner of his room. Watching him. William tried to tell his mom about the shadow man when he was little, but she just made a big deal of looking under the bed and in the closet and declaring it free of ghosts and monsters. All while the shadow man watched her.

It had been five years since the shadow man first showed up. Now William was almost fourteen, and the shadow man was as familiar to him as anyone else in his family. William did not mind him. He called him Mr. Stranger because no matter how much he asked, the shadow man would not tell William his name.

Until tonight. A heavy pressure gripping his chest woke him.

William fluttered his eyelashes open. He looked around in milky confusion, expecting to find his mother.

Instead, Mr. Stranger stood over him, right at the edge of his bed. William had never seen him move from his corner before. The shadow man had both hands pressed firmly against William's shoulders. His touch felt like water, wrapping around him to pull him under.

William wondered if he should be afraid. The half-asleep part of his brain could not quite accept that Mr. Stranger had moved at all. He had been a constant in William's life, as unquestionable and unmoving as the wallpaper. Uncertainty twisted in his gut.

"Mr. Stranger," he whispered. "What are you doing?" William pushed his shoulders up against the midnight fingers holding him down. But he could not budge.

Mr. Stranger only pushed him down harder.

Now William knew something was wrong. He squirmed and wrestled as he whimpered, "You're going to wake up my mom, and then we'll both be in trouble."

Those unblinking red eyes held his. Mr. Stranger reminded William of one his cats when it managed to corner a mouse.

"I am not," he said, in a voice that sounded like rock scraping on rock, "called Mr. Stranger."

William frowned. "Who are you?"

"I'm your future," he said. "Don't cry, now."

And then the shadow man burrowed his hands under the soft flesh of William's shoulders. He slipped under William's skin as if he were trying on a new coat.

William opened his mouth to scream, but nothing happened. His body wouldn't move. No matter how much he felt his own mind screaming at him to call for his mother, to kick, to run, to do anything at all, William lay there, frozen. Limp.

The shadow man kept burrowing into him. "I have been watching you all your life. I have been molding you to be my vessel." As he spoke, his voice warped and thinned. "And now you will be the shadow, and I will be William."

William felt himself split like an old sticker being peeled apart. One of those cold hands wrapped around the back of his throat as if from the inside and pushed.

William fell out of his body and into the open air. He tumbled across the floor. His head should have hit his nightstand, but instead he passed right through it, as if he was made of nothing.

William stared at his hands. His fingers were black shadow, darkness on darkness. He lifted his head. He recognized himself laying on that bed. A black cloud hovered over his body. Then his body's mouth opened like a mannequin, and the last of the shadow man consumed him.

William's body sat up in bed. His eyes were red now, gleaming. A crooked smile warped his face.

William watched, helplessly, as his body rose out of bed and walked right through him. Right to his desk, to pick up the pair of scissors he had left there.

The demon in the boy's skin tiptoed out into the hall. It held the scissors hidden behind its back. "Mom?" it called in William's voice. "Mom, I had a bad dream."

I watched your entire life
I know you more than anyone

I'm so proud of who you have become
But our time will soon be done
If you end it, you can finally rest
Because you didn't miss a single breath

SCAN THE CODE
FOR A SCARE

↓

STRANGER DANGER

I'll never forget the time Dylan drove me home.

It was a sticky-wet night in July, and we were coming home late from dinner at his parents' house. They lived almost an hour away.

We'd only been on three dates, but he'd invited me over to eat dinner with his family. It felt like kind of a big deal—I was so nervous that my palms were sweating.

But dinner turned out to be less awkward than I'd feared. Both his parents were so welcoming. They'd served a big family-style dinner and spent hours telling stories about when Dylan was a young kid. There was the time he'd rescued a bird that had flown into their bay window, and he'd nursed it back to health in their garage. And the time he "mowed" the entire lawn using a toy mower and cried when he looked at his handiwork only to see all the grass had "grown back." They even shared a story about him meeting a state senator and asking when she was going to get busy making school lunches taste better. All of this confirmed what I already suspected: Dylan was a great guy.

I was relieved I didn't have to share stories about my own upbringing. There weren't many to tell—at least not ones my parents ever shared with me. They both worked a lot. I'd pretty much been raised by my babysitter, Marilyn, an elderly woman who lived down the street.

The only things I remember about her was that she taught

me about table manners and something called "stranger danger." She watched a lot of those true crime shows on TV—I suspect that had something to do with it. I wasn't used to big family dinners with laughter and story time. Most nights I just heated up something frozen and ate in front of my laptop.

By the time dessert wrapped, I was shocked to see it was already 11:30 p.m. I'd promised my parents I would be home by midnight, and we were already running thirty minutes late. Despite their easygoing attitude about pretty much everything else, curfew was a big deal. They were adamant about not being woken up.

Dylan's parents offered to let me stay in the guest room and take me in the morning, but I'd been insistent on going home. We should have waited. But we didn't.

We were on that desolate highway deep into midnight. The windows were rolled down and the stereo was blaring. The lights of the dashboard made his knuckles glow red. There was nothing between us and the night but a long, flat expanse of desert. No other cars, no cell reception.

The road banked and curved. Dylan slowed to follow it. He was scoffing at something his dad had said during the senator story.

"I thought it was sweet," I protested. In response, Dylan's ears turned red.

He stopped talking then, his focus tunneled out the windshield. I followed his gaze.

There. Something lay in the middle of the road, unmoving. It was huge and impossible to tell in the dark. Maybe a deer that had failed to outrace a truck?

And yet, it didn't look like a deer. It seemed too large, too ominous somehow. I squinted into the darkness, and the shadow moved. As it did, it seemed to get larger and larger. I was suddenly sure it wasn't a deer. My stomach crept into my throat.

As Dylan slammed his foot to the floor, brakes whining, I jammed the lock button on my door. "Hey, uhhh, Dylan? What are you doing?"

"I think she's hurt."

"The . . . animal?" I asked. "Um, I don't mean to be rude, but I'm already running late for curfew."

I didn't tell him that this animal, or whatever it was, seriously creeped me out. I didn't want him—the animal lover—to think I was a bad person. But I couldn't shake the feeling that this was not something you should stop for.

Run, my instincts flared. I shoved the thought aside and clenched my jaw.

Dylan looked at me like my priorities were seriously out of whack. "You should look again."

And as I looked, whatever it was moved again.

What I had mistaken for animal hide was an ill-fitting brown dress in tatters, with pieces of something hanging from its arms. As it pushed itself up, I realized the thing in the road was a woman. Her dark hair was wild and snared with leaves and sticks, as if it hadn't been washed for weeks.

But her eyes were empty black wells, staring at us. There was no fear in them. No hurt. Only hate and hunger. She tipped her head, questioning, were we going to help her? She raised an arm. Was there a hand at the end or just tattered fabric flapping? I couldn't tell.

I rolled my window up. Huge boulders sat on the right shoulder of the road. I imagined what could be behind them. This seemed like a trap, but maybe I was just being dramatic. Too many horror movies.

If there was one thing I'd learned this evening, it was that Dylan was a good person. Of course, he'd want to help someone in need. But something inside me told me to drive away immediately and never look back. *Stranger danger.* The thought echoed in my mind, like Marilyn herself had come back from the grave just to warn me. I swallowed hard.

Dylan put the car into Park. The shape started to move toward us.

"We need to go," I insisted, my voice rising. "Now."

"Are you kidding? Who knows when someone will come by again?" He threw open his door and began to step out of the car. "We're not just abandoning someone out here."

I reached for his hand. "Wait," I started, my voice lodging in my throat.

But Dylan shook my hand off and gave me his easy, perfect smile. "Relax. I'll be right back." I took a deep breath. Of course he was right. We couldn't just leave someone out in the middle of nowhere. How could I forgive myself if I discovered that someone had been found dead out here?

I barely kept myself from yelling at him to come back. But my knees were shaking. I had to press them together to keep them still.

Dylan approached the woman, who slowly stood up, revealing her true height, towering over Dylan. She must've been eight feet tall. I'd never seen a human loom so large.

If she was even human at all.

The pit in my stomach yawned, and I stifled a scream. Part of me almost flung my door open and dragged him back myself. But the bigger part of me was glued to the spot, knowing the only thing that separated me from *it* was a hunk of metal and a pane of glass.

She grabbed him by the shirt and lifted him to her face. Dylan's eyes turned to me, helpless. *Stranger danger*, my mind blared.

Dylan's expression was a mixture of surprise and fear and anguish.

"DYLAN!" I screamed uselessly, for it was already too late.

In one swift move like a kid snarfing licorice, the creature devoured everything above Dylan's waist. She tossed what remained of him to the side. Reflexively, I looked at the rest of him. Just a jumble of limbs and a bit of torso. His foot twitched, and I squeezed my eyes shut.

I decided then and there I would not die that night. No matter what it took.

Then her neck snapped toward me.

SCAN THE CODE
FOR A SCARE
↓

THE REAPING

I don't notice the thorn until the shock of it bites through my finger.

I stare at the rose in my hand like it's betrayed me. A single missed thorn on a rose stem that should have been thornless.

Blood beads from my fingertip. Instinctively, I stick my finger in my mouth and suck down the surprising tang of copper.

Ahead of me, the priest keeps droning on. Beside the priest, Nancy Wu's junior prom picture beams at us. Crystals gleam in her dark hair. She looks perfect and obnoxious, which feels true to life. What a shame to have lost her life so young.

And it is a shame, I try to tell myself, as I watch Mrs. Wu sob in the front row. There is a home with a hole in it now. A mother without her daughter. I do my best to feel bad. But even as I stare at the back of Mrs. Wu's head, I can't stop seeing Nancy Wu's grin in the seventh grade when I found the fat wad of chewing gum she'd stuck in my hair. All the countless times she tormented and humiliated me.

Truthfully, my sympathy is just as dead as Nancy.

I wipe my finger on my dress. The casket ahead of us is closed. I suppose they can't keep it open, after the way they found her. I can't imagine anybody looks too pretty after four days baking under the California sun. They found her out in national park country, bludgeoned.

A horrible tragedy, really.

I keep my stare pinned over the priest's shoulder. The sky overhead churns darkly. It might rain soon.

It's a thin crowd. For the first few dead kids, almost everyone turned up. The school and the town mourned together. But as the deaths mounted, fewer and fewer people went to the funerals. It was too exhausting, all this mourning and loss. Instead of condolences and shared grief, the town began exchanging whispers: How could so many teenagers from a sleepy little mountain town wind up dead? There were seven of them now. All six feet under. And no explanation, no trace of a killer. It put people on edge.

Except for me. I've been to every single funeral. Every eulogy, every candlelight vigil. Hoping to catch another fleeting glimpse of him: the dark one. The one who walks with the night, who will find us all in the end.

He's the reason I've done all of it.

You might know him as the Grim Reaper. I know him as the object of my affection.

I first saw him the day my family's dog died, standing in the corner of my living room. Waiting. I had never seen someone so beautiful. He wore a black cloak wrapped around his shoulders. But it was his face—his amber eyes—that penetrated me to my core. Through my tears, his gaze had touched mine, and he knew that I could see him. The look of surprise was instantaneous. It was mixed with a touch of amusement and, perhaps, delight.

I knew in that moment, as I know now, that we were connected like no other souls in the universe could be. That we were meant to be together for eternity.

The priest carries on, but I no longer listen. I can only stare, transfixed, at the being hovering behind him.

No one else at the funeral sees him. If they could, they would scramble in a mad panic.

The Reaper is a shadow lurking behind the priest. The fierce heat of his amber eyes hold mine once again. The lord of the afterlife is young. He looks no older than seventeen. And though he is as ageless as time, the handsome curve of his jawline still makes my breath catch.

He leans wearily on his scythe and nods his head sideways. An easy-enough message: *Follow.*

I barely notice the priest or the rest of the funeralgoers. I rise, entranced, trailing the Grim Reaper's dark path. No matter how often we do this, I am still dizzy.

He leads me to a stand of oak trees, just out of sight of the other mourners.

"What's this all about?" he snaps.

I scowl. "Odd way to say you missed me."

"I don't know what your plan is. But this is the seventh body." His face softens with his voice. "You know they'll catch you soon."

I puff myself up. Part of me wants to retort, "So what if they do?" The faster they catch me, the closer I'll be to my own reaping, that blissful moment when we can finally be together.

But the bigger part of me is angry that he's still playing dumb. That he's still pretending he doesn't know we're made for each other. Every fiber in my being wants to scream: "Can't you tell I've loved you since the moment I saw you?"

My finger pulses where the rose pierced me. I can only manage to say, "I've just wanted to see you."

The Reaper scoffs. He looks so very alive for a keeper of the dead. "Is that what this is all about?" He reaches out and cups my cheek in his palm. His touch is like fog and night. Then he gives me a graveyard smile. "Life is too precious for that."

Life. That fleeting pulse in between the beginning of existence and the rest of eternity. It feels like such a joke in comparison to my destiny.

For a moment, I can see Nancy's eyes widen in horror when I swing the rock at her. I'm the last thing she ever saw before entering her own eternity.

I'm the rose's hidden thorn.

At this, the Reaper sighs. He turns and begins to walk away. "The date of your reaping is written in the stars. Nothing you do can change it. No matter how many bodies mount."

My nostrils flare as the cool air whips at my bare legs.

"But I want to be with you," I call after him. I've never said the words out loud before, but now the weight of them hangs between us. "I won't stop—not if this is the only way we can be together."

The Reaper stops in his tracks and pierces me with a look I've never seen before. "You don't love me," he says. "You only think you do. You must stop this nonsense before any others wind up at my door."

I smile and tell the Reaper, "You don't know what I love."

I'm faithful to the dark
So follow me into the park
No, this isn't a dream
Shh . . . now quiet your scream.

SCAN THE CODE
FOR A SCARE

This is only the beginning
These are only just a few
The darkness is out there
And it's coming . . . for you